# Jarod
and the
# Mystery
of the
# Petroglyphs

A National Park Adventure Series Book

# Jarod and the Mystery of the Petroglyphs

Janice J. Beaty

SUNSTONE PRESS

SANTA FE

Sunstone books may be purchased for educational, business, or sales promotional use.
For information please write: Special Markets Department, Sunstone Press,
P.O. Box 2321, Santa Fe, New Mexico 87504-2321.

Cover Illustration and drawings by Lillian C. Beaty
Book and cover design › Vicki Ahl
Body typeface › Maiandra GD
Printed on acid-free paper
∞
eBook 978-1-61139-386-6

---

Library of Congress Cataloging-in-Publication Data

Beaty, Janice J.
  Jarod and the mystery of the petroglyphs : a National Park adventure series book / by Janice
J. Beaty ; Illustrations by Lillian C. Beaty.
      pages cm
  Summary: "Jarod becomes involved with ancient rock art mysteries in Petroglyph National
Monument in New Mexico and in other National Parks"-- Provided by publisher.
  Includes bibliographical references.
  ISBN 978-1-63293-071-2 (softcover : alk. paper)
  1.  Petroglyph National Monument (N.M.)--Juvenile fiction. [1. Petroglyph
National Monument (N.M.)--Fiction. 2. Brothers--Fiction. 3. Psychic ability--Fiction. 4. Adventure
and adventurers--Fiction.] I. Beaty, Lillian C. illustrator. II. Title.
  PZ7.1.B4344Jav 2015
  [Fic]--dc23
                                         2015017623

---

**WWW.SUNSTONEPRESS.COM**
SUNSTONE PRESS / POST OFFICE BOX 2321 / SANTA FE, NM 87504-2321 /USA
(505) 988-4418 / ORDERS ONLY (800) 243-5644 / FAX (505) 988-1025

To:

## Barb Taylor
Terrific Traveling
Companion

# Preface

Jarod Freeman, an *indigo child* with psychic abilities and his older brother Darrell, the narrator of this story, continue their adventures in the national parks of the Southwest while their mother paints illustrations for a book on the Indian rock art known as *petroglyphs*. Beginning in Petroglyph National Monument outside of Albuquerque, New Mexico, the boys are surprised by the number of these ancient drawings pecked out on the black volcanic rocks of the Monument. Who made them? What do they say? Can Jarod really interpret their meanings?

As they clamber over the black boulders, Jarod actually meets the live snake pictured on his rock, "a rattlesnake, fer gosh sakes!" sputters Darrell. But then Darrell meets another lively investigator, Omega, who seems to know more about rock art than Jarod, and informs him she is coming along in their vintage orange VW camper bus. Another *indigo*? "Wouldn't cha know it?" grumbles Darrell.

Their petroglyph trail takes them up to Dinosaur National Monument in Utah where life-size petroglyphs of strange, real people, the Fremonts, have important messages for the boys about stabilizing the Earth during these unstable times. Then on down to Capitol Reef National Park they go where the ancient Fremonts were first discovered. "Baddies" trying to steal the boys' buzzing knife and Omega's talking necklace, remain hot on their trail to the end.

My own fascination with Southwestern petrolglyphs began long ago in Buckeye, Arizona during the weekends we spent searching for rock art panels. But the boys' fictional search opened new doors for my own understanding of what these ancient drawings have to tell us. Want to come along? Hop aboard for the ride of your life!

—Janice J. Beaty

# 1

# Black Mesa

Hello! I'm Darrell Freeman. The older brother of Jarod, the little squirt who see's-all and know's-all from the story he had me tell about the Joshua Trees in a previous adventure. Why can't he tell his own stories? I know. He just wants me to take all the blame for the wacky things he says. Yup. This time he really has blown the lid off the peanut butter jar! You know it!

Do you know what petroglyphs (**pet-**tro-glifs) are? They are ancient markings or pictures or whatever on rocks. You find them all over the world. Well, maybe not you, but somebody finds them all over the world. In this country they are mostly in the Southwest.

Now don't get upset if you live in the Northwest, or Southeast, or Upstate New York, or wherever. They are there, too. But in California, Nevada, Texas, Arizona, New Mexico, Colorado, and Utah there are so many more of them. Especially in Utah.

Utah is the all-round, hands-down, petroglyphical capital of America. Who says so? Me. Darrell Freeman, the most all-round, top-of-the-heap, petroglyphical, flat-face rock finder in the U.S.of A.! Just ask anybody. (Trust me.)

Why are there so many petroglyphs in Utah? I guess it's because there are so many flat-faced rocks in Utah. You have to have rocks to have petroglyphs. You know, big rocks with flat faces that you can peck out pictures on. Petroglyphs need flat surfaces for pecking and drawing. And they need hot weather and dryness to keep them looking good for hundreds of years, even thousands of years. You know it.

Utah is one of the hottest, driest places you will ever run into (or out of). Trust me. So where did we start our search for petroglyphs? At Petroglyph National Monument in New Mexico! Wouldn't ya know it? (What can I say?)

The "we" in this story is my mom the painter and book illustrator and my ten-year-old brother, Jarod (I call him Jay-Rod), the so-called "indigo child." I didn't call him that. It came from psychologists, I guess. They say that many children born after 1982 have special gifts of seeing things and knowing things that most of us don't have.

The color indigo blue shows up in their "aura," says my mom (whatever that means). And some of them, like Jarod, also have ADHD. You know, that attention deficit hyperactivity disorder. Jarod may be disorderly (whew!), but he sure isn't disordered. You should be around him and you'd soon find out. He's the smartest kid I ever met. He knows all kinds of things that no one ever taught him. Except sitting still. Who-ee!

Just look at him now scrambling up between two humungous black boulders on the mesa side over there. He's yelling that he's found a new petroglyph of a parrot—a macaw from Mexico, he says. (How does he know that?)

Get used to that word "petroglyph" (**pet**-tro-glif), because you will really have to loosen up your tongue on it before you try some of the other tongue-twisters Jarod uses.

I'm talking about the word he uses for the rock pictures of people, don't ya know. Scientists that study such things call people-like figures "anthropomorphs"… (**an**-thro-po-morfs). Wouldn't ya know it? Gotcha, didn't I?

"Why can't they just say "man," or "woman," or "person," for gosh sakes, and get over it?" I asked Jarod.

He says it's because sometimes these people-figures have heads like birds or animals and claws for hands or feet. And sometimes they don't even have a head—or feet. Hmmm. I really think it's because those scientists don't know what they are. So they call them anthropomorphs to cover all their bases. Who's going to argue about a bird-headed, claw-footed man that's called an anthropomorth? Sounds real scientific, doesn't it? But let's us not get so tongue-twisted at the beginning of our adventure. Let's just call them "anthros." So we do.

Of course, at Black Mesa where we are now there aren't that many anthros. Wouldn't ya know it? Just the same, we started our search for Southwestern glyphs here at this petroglyph park west of the city of Albuquerque, New Mexico. You should see it! All these big black volcanic boulders are strewn along the sides of a mesa wall for seventeen miles. Yup.

The wall drops down to a flat valley floor that the city of Albuquerque sits on. Looks like some giant cleared off the flat mesa top and pushed the black rock rubbish over the side. Only, the rocks aren't rubbish. Far from it. They're sacred. Yup. To the Indians these rocks and this site are all sacred—like an open-air church, you could say.

"Most Anglos (white people) don't understand the importance of petroglyphs to native people," says Jay-Rod. "They don't know that each petroglyph here was pecked through the black surface of the rocks long ago to record something spiritual. This site is where long-ago Indians connected with their gods." Whoa!

I found out there's supposed to be 17,000 petroglyphs here! Whew! Who counted 'em? They can't all be sacred, can they, I asked Jay-Rod?

"They are," said Jay. "They were made by the holy men from villages that once stood around here from about 1300 AD to 1500 AD. For hundreds of years holy people came to this same site and pecked their pictures and signs."

How does he know all this? I asked Mom, and she said he's right. Then she read to me what one of the modern-day Indians had to say about this site:

> The petroglyph area is where messages to the spirit world are communicated. We consider each of these petroglyphs to be a record of visions written here of some spiritual being, event, or expression.

Most Anglos don't know this. They think the Indians were just doodling or putting their names or graffiti on the rocks when they passed by. Wouldn't ya know it? That's what Anglos would do, not Indians. Indians took their rock writing seriously. And they take all these black volcanic rocks seriously, too.

Did you know native people believe that rocks (and all things) are alive? They do. And so does my brother Jay-Rod. That's how he finds out about them. He talks with them. Hoo-boy!

The city of Albuquerque runs almost up to the mesa wall in some spots. Pretty cool to have your house on a street that runs right up to petroglyph rocks, wouldn't ya say? Well, maybe you wouldn't. Where we are right now, like I said, is Petroglyph National Monument, set up to preserve the petroglyphs for people to see them. Also to protect them from vandalism.

There's a Visitor Center here and three little canyons with trails to follow. Mom has a commission to paint petroglyphs for a book being written about them. She and Dad (when he was alive) used to come out here to Albuquerque in the summer and hike around the mesa wall to see how many different kinds they could find. That's how come they bought our vintage Volkswagen camper bus in the first place—to camp in on their expeditions.

This bus is really a stand-out. Folding table in back, for poker games, (just kidding)—refrigerator for tons of sodas and chips, (scratch that one)—a padded way-back area to stretch out on for boring road stretches, and where Mom sleeps at night—and of course, a roof poptop that pops up at night to sleep in.

There's also a stand-up tent that we can hitch to the open side door for an extra room. Sometimes it just stands by itself to anchor down our camping spot when we are out driving. Oh, yeah and the front bus doors have a decal of a roadrunner bird on them. That's what we call the bus: "The Roadrunner." Cool, huh?

But I almost forgot the most stand-outish thing about our bus is its color. It's *orange*! Yup. How could I forget that? "Orange marmalade," we call it. Makes it pretty easy to keep track of when we're out tramping around the desert. But makes it pretty hard to hide when there's bad dudes around. You know it!

I get to drive the bus around the area while Mom is painting! Yippee! We can go almost anywhere in the parks we visit as long as I call in our whereabouts on my cell phone. Double-cool, huh?

But now the call I hear is coming from up behind another of those big black boulders. It's Jay-Rod talking without moving his lips. He's saying: "Darry, come quick. I'm entertaining an interesting visitor up here! But go easy. Don't make any noise! And don't come too close or he might smell you."

That must mean trouble, since Jay-Rod only talks without moving his lips in emergencies. I scramble as silently as I can up the slope between the boulders. There is Jay-Rod sitting statue-still on a good-size rock and staring down. There on the ground at the base of the rock is a big old coiled up snake. A rattlesnake staring up at Jay-Rod and flicking its tongue, but not rattling! A rattlesnake! Forgoshsakes!

Jay-Rod has this weird ability of attracting wild critters of all kinds without doing anything. Birds come and sit on his finger (or head). Jackrabbits hop right up and stare him in the face. Prairie dogs pop out of their holes and scamper over to see him. But rattlesnakes? That is something new. Now he continues talking to me without moving his lips while staring at the snake and not moving a muscle.

"He's checking me out, Darry. I guess I'm sitting on the roof of his house. See his tongue flicking in and out? That's his "olfactory nerve." That's how he smells. Don't let him get a whiff of you, or he's sure to get riled up. Just cool it. He's going to go back under the rock when he feels it's safe."

That's my brother Jay-Rod. Not an ounce of fear with a yard-long rattlesnake coiled a few inches below his dangling feet. Oh-wow! And sure enough, the snake does uncoil itself as smooth as a yo-yo and slithers back under the rock. Whew!

Jay-Rod waits a few seconds before pulling himself upright on top of the rock. Then he does a little jig and jumps over to the next boulder. I was hoping there wasn't a snake under that one, too. No. But as he soon points out, there is a snake *on* it: a snake petroglyph!

"I've counted five of them on this slope, Darry. Some of them with horns. The ancient people really respected snakes, you know. Snakes were symbols of death and rebirth for them because they shed their skins and became new all over again. Did ya know that, Darry? We are on an ancient snake ground. That's why you see so many snake petroglyphs around here. The shamans—you know, the holy medicine men—the ones that pecked out the images of snakes onto these rocks, used snake energy to travel between life and death."

"Okay, Bro, if you say so. But let's get out of here for now. My olfactory nerves are not as cool as yours. I think they're beginning to crumble, if ya wanna know. C'mon! Let's go!"

So down we both scrambled, over and around the black boulders to the sandy trail at the bottom. And wouldn't ya know it, right there at the trailhead is a park sign with a picture of a rattlesnake and a warning that neither of us had bothered to read:

*Rattlesnakes may be found in this area. They are important members of the natural community. They will not attack. But if disturbed or cornered, they will defend themselves. Give them distance and respect.*

Now I read it. Jay-Rod didn't have to. He already knew what it said. My response: "Don't tell Mom!" So that was our first morning in Petroglyph National Monument.

Before we could go on our way, Jay-Rod suddenly turned around, looked up the slope toward the rock he'd been sitting on, and had this to say: "Darry, we have to come back. I said this was a snake ground, but it's more than that. It's a sacred ground where snake ceremonies were performed. That snake thought I might be one of the snake kachinas, believe it or not!"

Whoa! There he goes again with those words. What in the sneakie-snakie universe is a kachina? (kaht-**chee**-nah) That did it! I should have known better than to ask Mr. Know-It-All a question like that. His encyclopedia of knowledge about kachinas suddenly poured out.

"The first kachinas were thought to be gods by the Pueblo people. They came from the stars and were much taller and better looking than the Puebloans. Yes, you could say they were ETs. You know, extraterrestrials. Each one came to help and protect a certain animal or bird or plant."

Jay-Rod was on a roll: "There was a snake kachina and a bird kachina and a plant kachina, to name a few. And especially, rain kachinas in this desert land. They stayed for awhile and taught the people how to take care of their special nature objects. Then they left. After that certain clans of people took over their jobs.

"A person from each of those groups would dress up like the kachina and become that kachina for maybe a year. They would have sacred dances at the Pueblo villages to celebrate and honor those kachinas.

"And guess what, Darry? Pueblo people still live in villages along the Rio Grande River here in New Mexico even today. And these people still honor the kachinas in the same way."

Whoa! Was he putting me on? A snake kachina? A yard-long rattlesnake thought my little brother might be a snake god? The idea left me ready to roll in the sand shaking with laughter. That is, if the ground was clear of snakes.

What are you going to do with a kid like that who believes that everything on Earth is alive and can communicate with you? He also believes that all of us humans are "Mighty Spiritual Beings" trapped in human bodies. All of us have the same powers as he does, but we don't "re-member" how to use them. He also says that he and all the other so-called "indigo children" are here to help us "re-member."

"It's time to wake up," he says, "and re-member who we are." Okay. I don't mind being a Mighty Spiritual Being. In fact, it's pretty cool. But communicating with a snake? No way!

"Why do we have to come back here, Jay-Rod, to this snakie place? You already had your little chit-chat with the reptile. And I'm certainly not going to add my tongue-wiggles. Can't ya just see it? It's enough to bring on a song.

> Where, oh where can my rattlesnake be?
> Where, oh where can he be?
> With his tail a-skitter
> And his tongue a-flitter
> Let's hope he doesn't see me!

You know me: always singing and reciting poetry (mostly my own, I'm sorry to say) when things get sticky. But then I noticed something else: "Say, wait a minute, Jay-Rod? Where's your backpack? Did you leave it somewhere again? Maybe up there at that snake rock? You better go back and get it right away." He was always leaving something somewhere.

"Take it easy, Darry. I think we both should spend some more time in this little canyon. Maybe we can learn more about the kachinas whose petroglyphs are here. And besides, Mom asked you to take some photos with your cell phone camera. Did you?"

Of course I didn't. That first trail, Mesa Point Trail, was a steep one. I was really out of shape after goofing off all winter. So there I was huffing and puffing my way to the top of the mesa wall. The slope was covered all over with black boulders as thick as chicken pox on an oyster.

The petroglyphs were not pecked on every rock, thank the universe—only scattered here and there. So it was sort of like a treasure hunt to find them. Here a glyph, there a glyph, everywhere a glyph, glyph. So no, I didn't take any pictures the first time through.

Jay Rod, of course, didn't stay on the trail like he was supposed to either. I tried to keep an eye on him while scanning the rocks for petroglyphs, but both things soon got away from me! I only hoped he could find his backpack. This time though, I would take photos for Mom of any glyphs that looked outstanding. Trouble was, they all did! Meanwhile, let the great kachina of the Rio Grande keep Jay-Rod from falling off the steep walls of Black Mesa!

He almost did. I was right to the end of Mesa Point Trail when this hefty-looking guy in a black T-shirt with a white skull on it came stomping along dragging a struggling Jay-Rod by the arm. I secretly took their picture.

"Hey, kid," he growled at me. "This nosy little nit-wit belong to you? He was trying to steal something from my backpack when I wasn't looking. Caught him just in time."

"Darry," Jay sputtered out between gasps of breath. "He broke into my backpack where I left it on the trail and took our Dad's hunting knife! I was just trying to get it back."

Quick-thinking me put out my hand to shake hands with the man, so he would let loose of Jay-Rod. "Hi, I'm Darrell Freeman, Junior, and what did you say your name was mister?" The man turned Jay loose and muttered, "Russell."

"So your name or initials would be on the knife, if it belongs to you, wouldn't it, Mr. Russell? Or our Dad's would be, if it was our knife. So let's see the knife." Nobody made a move. I grabbed Jay's backpack and dumped it out. Nothing but a peanut butter sandwich, half-eaten, an empty water bottle, and his wind-breaker.

The man finally dug through his pack and threw a hunting knife out on the ground. Sure enough, it had D. F. on the handle just where I carved it. "Oh, that is our knife. Thanks. Guess it was just a mix-up. My brother is noted for getting things mixed up. Hope you can find your knife, mister."

I quickly put the knife in Jay's pack and hustled him down the trail toward our camper bus. "Keep walking and don't look back. If we hear him coming after us, we'll run," I hissed.

# 2

# Omega

Once in the bus we both let out a huge sigh. That knife had a real history. It was not ours at first. It belonged to a woman in a black SUV at Joshua Tree National Park last summer who had threatened Jay-Rod with it while she was trying to steal his famous buzzing rock. (Read-all-about-it in *Jarod and the Mystery of the Joshua Trees*).

She dropped it by accident when she rushed off with a piece of Jay's foolsgold by mistake—instead of the rock she really wanted. Now Jay's buzzing rock was safely buried in a secret spot in Joshua Tree National Park.

We were keeping the knife for our own. I carved my initials on it. Saying we had our Dad's initials was just my trick to let the guy think we had a man back at our camp to defend us. Dad's initials were the same as mine.

Who was that guy, anyway? Why was he trying to get our knife? How did he know about it? Neither Jay-Rod or I could come up with anything. Here we go again, I thought to myself. Just like back in Joshua Tree with certain people trying all the time to get our buzzing rock for some unknown reason. Now, would we have the same problem with the knife? Why would anyone want an old hunting knife?

But before I got carried away any further, Mom appeared with her painting stuff in hand ready to drive us back to the campground. Hurray! I was starving! Should have kept my mouth shut. Whenever anyone in our family shows any excitement about anything, they are the one who gets chosen to do the thing. Of course, that meant me. I would be the fire starter tonight. That meant gathering wood, chopping it down to size, arranging it in a fire pit, and starting it. And no fair using newspapers!

Okay. I would show everybody what an expert fire maker I was. Back at camp I swiftly gathered up an armload of wood, chopped it up, and piled kindling against a log with a flourish. Then I started shaving off some tinder from one of the pieces.

"Hey! What's going on here? Is this hunting knife dull, or what? Every time I press down on it to cut off some shavings it slips out of my hand. Look. Yup, did it again."

This sent Jay-Rod into spasms of laughter. He told Mom I was so nervous about seeing a snake in the park that my hand was shaking too hard to cut the wood. I flipped the knife over to him with a snicker. "Okay, mister smarty-pants. You do it."

You should have seen the look on his face when the knife wouldn't work for him either! Then he held it up to his ear. What's with him, anyway? Did he expect a knife to talk like a petroglyph? He must have talking objects on the brain! But after a minute the smile on his face vanished.

"Listen, Darry, and see what you think." I held the knife up to my ear, too. Omygosh! The knife blade was buzzing—just like that crazy rock in Joshua Tree Park! Here we go again!

Next day Mom printed off my photos on her computer, so she could choose which ones to paint next. She must have seen the one of Jay-Rod and the man, but didn't say anything. Jay-Rod looked them over too. He took the one of himself and the man and hid it somewhere. Then he looked to see which rock he would meditate on next. To meditate he would sit down in front of the petroglyph, close his eyes, and listen to what it had to say.

"Darry, I get the distinct feeling we will receive an important message from one of these petroglyphs," he informed me.

Hoo-boy! Did I want to hear that? Another message from a rock, telling us what we had to do. Most of the rocks here were from two to four feet tall. The petroglyphs on them were anywhere from six inches to a couple of feet in height. A lot bigger than the ones we saw in Joshua Tree Park. After finding the right photo Jay-Rod would have to go find the rock. Meditating on a photo didn't work for him.

I was wondering how he was going to choose. Jay always does things so completely different than anybody else. Yup. He started by spreading out all the photos on the table in the back of the bus and checking them over. Then he moved them around like chess players on a chessboard. Finally he picked up one and held it in front of his face. Was he going to hold it up against his ear to see if it buzzed? (My little joke.). But he did hold it face down on his forehead between his eyes. He called that spot his "third eye." Oh, man-o-man!

"Okay, Bro. This is the one," he finally decided. "You pick yours and then we're off to Mesa Point Trail."

He showed me his photo. It had three figures: two parrots facing each other while attached at their stomachs, an eagle feather headdress with an arrow sticking up from one side, and a four-pointed star, all of them in a row. Wow! I remembered that one and almost chose it myself as a special rock for Mom. A spread of petroglyphs like that across the face of a rock is called a "panel," she told us..

My choice was a favorite of both of us: a glyph of a macaw parrot in a cage tipped on its side in a down position. Beside it was a macaw standing free with a wing up and its tail feathers spread. It was really cool. That glyph was on the Macaw Trail, naturally.

"Good choice, Bro. That's a picture of the same bird twice, you know," said Jay-Rod. "First where he's in a cage, and next where he's been let out. Lots of panels show the same figure over and over as the figure does different things—like in a comic strip without the dividing lines. And by the way, that's a bird shaman's messenger. The macaw, I mean. He let it out of its cage to carry a message. So find out what the message is, if you can."

How does he know all these things? My brother, the whiz—or wizard, if you ask me. Next he told me what I should do when I found the rock again. Sit on the ground in front of it with my legs crossed. Stare at the petroglyph until I knew it by heart. Then close my eyes and meditate. Blank out all thoughts and wait until something came into my mind. Uuh!

"Okay. But just don't take that hunting knife with you this time, Jay-Rod. Hide it up in the bus poptop like you did with the buzzing rock in Joshua Tree Park. And let me know if that guy comes around again. Have you got your cell phone with you?"

Meanwhile, Mom set up her easel over on one side of the Mesa Point Trail with the photo of the petroglyph she was going to paint clipped to it. "Ten o'clock sharp, boys," she reminded us. "Then we're on our way again!"

The trouble with me was I couldn't make myself sit on the ground in front of the petroglyph. It seemed like a dumb thing to do. I'm such a tall gangly kid I would look like a string bean all scrunched up. Anyway, I was too old to do such little-kid things. What would people think if they saw me? Jay-Rod never minded what anyone thought about him, but I did. All right, for Jay's sake I would try it.

I waited until there were no people nearby and sat down. But then I got up right away. What about snakes? I poked around the rock and the ones next to it. Nothing. Well, maybe the bird shaman would keep the snakes away. Still I couldn't make myself sit back down. So I stood there facing the rock with my eyes closed for a while—quite a while. Then somebody poked me in the back. I really jumped!

"Hey, that's my back! What'd'ya think you're doing? D'ya think I'm some kind of pincushion (whatever they are)?"

I whirled around and faced—yikes! A girl! A little girl about Jay's age, dressed like an Indian with a feather in her long black hair and a hand with only three fingers! Where did she come from? Bad idea to ask, I soon found out. Once she got started talking, she couldn't seem to shut up. Uuh!

It turns out she was camping with her mother, too, over in our campground. She said her name was Omega, and that she was an indigo child!!! Oh, man-o-man! Where do they all come from? She wanted to know what was I doing standing in front of that rock with my eyes closed? Did the bird speak to me? Was I having a vision quest? And on and on. Then she dashed up the trail and out of sight without waiting for my answers. Whoa!

Then my cell phone rang. It was Mom wondering where I was and did I forget we were going to leave at ten sharp? Okay, okay. I would be there as soon as I could find my way out of this rocky maze. Amazing!

First I found Jay. He wanted to know if Omega had found me? What? How could she have been way over to Mesa Point Trail where Jay-Rod was and then way back to Macaw Trail where I was in such a short time? Anyway, how did he know her? Oh, yeah. He always said indigo children recognize each other right off the bat handle. Talking about bats, she was the batty one, for sure. Then he let loose the bombshell.

Omega was coming with us! What? Yes. She and her mother were visiting friends in Albuquerque before they returned to their home up in Aztec, New Mexico. But since we were on our way in that direction her mother asked our mother if Omega could ride with us. We could drop her off at Aztec Ruins National Monument where her father worked. Her mother thought she'd have a much better time with us two boys than with her. Hmm. Or was her mother just trying to get rid of her? (My stupid thought, of course.)

She was Jay-Rod's age, but acted a lot younger. Then she would suddenly change her tune and act just like a grown-up. I thought the whole thing was an act. We'd never get to know the real Omega. If she could only keep her mouth shut.

She didn't bother Jay-Rod at all. He was used to all kinds of people trying to tell him what to do or what not to do. Sometimes he paid attention to them, sometimes not. Usually he just went on his own cheerful way—no matter what other people tried to make him do.

Later when Omega got mad at him, he just grinned at her. If she tried to take one of his "collectibles," he just calmly took it back and put it away. Once she dumped out an ant farm he was starting in a jar. Did that bother him? Nope. He just started collecting tarantulas instead. (Mom dumped them out!)

But finally he said to her, quite strongly for Jay-Rod: "We're on a secret mission to save the Earth from the damage people are doing to it. The petroglyphs are helping us. Are you with us or not?" After that she calmed down a little. She began collecting soil samples in plastic baggies and giving them to Jay-Rod with her three-fingered hand. What a ding-bat!

He thanked her for the soil, but told her she could be more useful if she would help us when we got to her place in Aztec, New Mexico—that is, if she could keep our secret. We'll see,

The road north went faster than our bus did. 70, 75, 80 mph, across a desert full of— nothing . No Joshua Trees here. Not even much sage. Only signs for entering and leaving Indian reservations: San Felipe, Santo Domingo, San Ildefonso, Tesuque, Pojoaque. No signs of people except at the casinos. Indians have casinos these days! Imagine it! A great trick to play on the white man who has cheated them from the start, was my opinion. Oh, yeah, I forgot Santa Fe—a city, of course. We sped through that and on up north through mountainous country.

By mid-afternoon we made it north as far as the town of Taos. What a place! You come up, up a mountain road from down at the bottom of a canyon along the Rio Grande River. Then the road takes a quick blind turn at the top. Suddenly, you feel like you're taking off through outer space! (I bet some reckless drivers do!) No more canyon walls. You're looking out over the whole world. Far below is the tiny river and a sagebrush desert sweeping away to forever. Taos is a little adobe town way over to the east at the foot of the Sangre de Christo Mountains. Whew!

Mom had a friend in Taos who lived out on the mesa north of town. So that's where we went for the night. Omega wanted to stop at the Taos Indian Pueblo, (She was dressed like an Indian, ya know), but Mom wouldn't. So she kept up this little-girl whining: "I wanna stop at Taos, I wanna stop at Taos, etc." until Mom turned up the radio. We finally got to Mom's friend's place and set up our tent. Then Mom said we could go out exploring with the bus as far down as the road with the blinking light. Explore what, I wondered? Nothing out here but sagebrush.

"Does that mean out to the bridge over the Rio Grande gorge?" Omega wanted to know. "Yes." She lightened up after that, especially after she found out I had a driver's license. I guess Omega knew her way around here. So off we went in our orange marmalade bus out to the gorge bridge.

Do you have any of fear of heights? If so, you better not get out of your car there and walk across that bridge. The mesa is flat as a skipping stone as far as you can see. You're driving along and have no idea you're anywhere near a sudden drop-off. A 1,000-foot-deep river gorge! If you do get out and look down: uuh! Your stomach feels like it might drop off, too!

"C'mon," yelled Omega after we parked. She dragged us right out to the middle of that flat bridge. You'd think you were standing in outer space looking down at the Earth from a space shuttle. Omygosh! Way down below was the little Rio Grande. You couldn't even see it clearly because the sun didn't reach to the bottom of that narrow canyon in late afternoon. Awesome!

As we collected our wits and realized what we were looking at, I suddenly got this funny feeling. No, it wasn't altitude sickness. It wasn't dizziness from fear of heights. It was something else. Omega looked at me and asked, "Do you feel it?" I'm pretty sure Jay-Rod was feeling something, too, the way he was dancing around.

It felt like I was sort of buzzing—vibrating all over; like some kind of energy was coming up from that deep, deep gorge and running right through me. Omega was laughing and shaking our hands and yelling, "You pass, you pass!" like it was some kind of test. I guess it was.

Afterward she said that not everybody could feel the gorge energy. Only fourth-density people like her and other indigos and a few others. She said the gorge was made by an ancient crack in the Earth. Yes, a fault. We knew about those, all right, from the faults around Joshua

Tree Park. I was also thinking about that rock energy Jay-Rod and me were carrying inside us from the Heart Rock at Joshua Tree Park (More on that later).

When we got back to our camp, we laid out our petroglyph pictures for Omega to look at.

"You're reading them all wrong. You're reading them like most Anglos (white people) do who look at words left-to-right in a line. Petroglyphs are a kind of picture communication—not writing. But the pictures mean different things than you thought. Most glyphs of big horned sheep don't stand for sheep at all. That's right. A lot of them stand for people and their travels. Yep. Their heads point in the direction people are traveling. The length of legs tells how long they traveled. If their feet are turned backwards it means the people went some place and then came back." Whoa!

Almost all the animals in our glyphs stood for people, she said. Oh-wow! She sounded exactly like a scientist who had studied petroglyphs for years. I was stunned. Suddenly, I knew running into Omega could be the best thing that ever happened to us.

She also said that most of the petroglyphs on Black Mesa were made by the Anasazi medicine men or shamans between 1300 and 1500 AD. That's Ah-nah-**sah-**zee, if you want to give it a try. The Pueblo people themselves don't use that Navajo word. They want their ancient people to be called Ancestral Puebloans.

Jay-Rod handed her the photo of the glyphs he was trying to make sense of. She didn't put it against her "third eye" or do any kind of meditating. She just looked at it and said the two macaw birds facing each other with their stomachs touching were a Hopi clan sign. That means they were probably one of the Anasazi clans, too, since the Hopi came from the Anasazi.

Double birds like that usually had something to do with rain. A lot of the ceremonies were performed to bring rain to this desert country, she told us. But they really weren't birds. They stood for a man, probably a shaman from the bird clan. The eagle feather headdress with an arrow coming out of it meant he should get ready for war, she said. The four-pointed star meant that he had the power of the Morning Star. Wow! Jay-Rod thought about it, but then decided she was probably right. Maybe petroglyphs mean different things to different people, I thought.

Then Omega looked at my photo of the macaw in the cage and the macaw standing free. She said the macaw also represented a person. Because it was a beautiful bird it probably stood for a pretty girl. Being in the cage meant the girl was being "confined" or "held back" in some way—not really in a cage. Then being out of the cage at the bottom showed the bird/girl was happy because she had been set free.

But Jay-Rod had told me the bird was a messenger and to look for the message. What did Omega think? She sort of blushed and walked away. I knew right away what that meant: she must have thought she was the bird-girl who had been restricted (by her mother?), and now she was free. The "message" had been standing right behind me at that rock when I had my eyes closed! But it wasn't for me. It was for Jay-Rod. Oh, man-o-man!

# 3

# UFO

Back at our camp as the sun when down, Jay-Rod built a huge fire. We all sat around it roasting hot dogs and marshmallows, telling stories and singing songs. Mine:

> Yippee, ki, yi, yo,
> Git along orange camper,
> It's your good fortune and lots of my own.
> Yippee, ki, yi, yo,
> Git along orange camper,
> For you know that Utah will be your new home! (Whenever!)

After the last song we could hear the coyotes answering. Mom's friend's house was an adobe out at the end of a dirt road. The sagebrush desert stretched clear over to the invisible Rio Grande gorge. But when it got really dark, oh-wow! I wasn't prepared for the night sky in this high desert country.

Even at Albuquerque there were too many city lights to see the stars real clear. But here! Omygosh! It looked like you could reach out and touch them. And there were so many! No wonder the ancient people drew stars and star-faces on the rocks.

That night Jay-Rod and me slept in the tent, with Omega in the poptop and Mom in the wayback of the bus as usual. It wasn't long before we felt stones hitting our tent. Oh, yeah, probably Miss Omega was scared of sleeping on top of the bus by herself like that. She wasn't going to come in with us I decided. (How do ya stop her?).

"What's this thing doing up in the poptop?" she wanted to know, as she entered our tent. "It's buzzing so loud, it's keeping me awake!" She tossed us the old hunting knife. Wouldn't ya know it! We had to tell her the whole story about Jay-Rod's buzzing rock from Joshua Tree Park—how a lady and a man tried to steal it from us—how the lady accidentally dropped her hunting knife—how we put it in Jay's backpack with the buzzing rock—and how we finally buried the rock—or rather it buried itself. The knife must have picked up energy from the rock to make it buzz like that.

"What kind of energy?" she wanted to know.

"That's what we don't know." Jay told her. " It's all a mystery to us. But we figure it has something to do with Earth energy and helping the Earth to settle down during this important time of change on the planet."

"Why would somebody try to steal the rock?"

"We didn't know that either," I continued. "And now a man down at the Albuquerque petroglyph park tried to steal that knife out of Jay's pack."

"See what kind of outlaws you've got yourself involved with, Omega," laughed Jay-Rod.

"Uh-huh, just my type."

Then without warning a bright light filled the tent. We carefully poked our heads out of the tent opening to see what it was. Omygosh! It was coming from a silver disk hanging in the night sky right over the Rio Grande! Could it really be? Yeah, it was! A real, live UFO!

Next morning Omega was the first one to say anything as we were packing up, getting ready to leave. "Well, what did you think about that?"

"What did we think about what?" I replied.

"You, know. About what happened last night."

"You mean about the buzzing knife?" I replied, knowing she didn't mean that.

"Oh, c'mon, you boys. You mean you don't remember about the UFO?"

I looked at Jay-Rod and he looked at me and shrugged. "Okay, Ms. Know-It-All, you tell us what you think about the UFO." I finally managed weakly.

"I can't believe you so-called Mighty Spiritual Beings don't remember about the UFO we all saw last night out over the gorge. The silver one with the floodlight sweeping across the mesa. It beamed us up! Don't you even remember that—being aboard the UFO?" We didn't answer.

At that moment Mom called us to climb aboard. We were finally ready to head out for Aztec, New Mexico, where Omega lived. Mom got to drive all by herself up front that morning. The three of us huddled in the back trying to recall in whispers the harebrained affair that Omega was talking about.

Being aboard a UFO? Had she lost her rocks? Even Jay-Rod with his instant ability to meditate and go within himself, had nary a clue. We thought she was putting us on. Making up this mind-boggling fairy-tale about being in the cabin of a UFO with extraterrestrials—ETs who were talking to us.

"They made you forget," she finally decided. "They blocked your memory."

"Blocked our memory? Why would they do that?" I asked in a sneering tone.

"Probably so you wouldn't be scared."

"Scared? Scared of what? Of them? Why would we be scared of ETs, whatever they are?"

Omega laughed. "Oh, yes, you would. If you've never been face-to-face with an ET, you would be scared, all right. I was, the first time. I couldn't believe what my eyes were showing me. There were these weird little gray guys with huge dark eyes. Their long skinny arms reached almost to their knees. My brain was ready to shut down. I almost passed out.

"Then they sort of shape-shifted to look more like people. But then they peeled back to look like themselves again. You'd be scared, all right. When they finally held up a hand in friendship, I saw it had only three fingers like mine. Then I wasn't scared."

ETs with three fingers? Hoo-boy! Where did she get such stuff? I looked over at Jay-Rod. I could see he was not about to laugh. His face was sort of frozen in an omygosh stare. Was he remembering something?

Omega pulled out Jay's buzzing knife from her backpack and handed it to me. She said she had it in her hand when the ETs beamed us up to their ship. But they took it from her at once. They didn't give it back until they sent us down again.

The minute my hand touched that knife, my mind sort of snapped open and out spilled everything. I could see and hear the whole scenario. It gave me goose bumps. I started to shake all over. She was right. We were in a cabin with ETs. Jay and me just sort of stood there like statues. Omega had this long talk with the little gray beings with their big black eyes.

They were telling her she needed to go all the way with us. All the way up to the petroglyphs in Utah. She needed to take the knife, too, and not let anybody steal it. The energy it contained was important. They didn't say what it was or why. We would know what to do with it when we found the right petroglyphs. They would keep track of us. But we would have to do the work ourselves. Then we would see them again.

Uuuh! We both sort of slumped back in total shock. I handed Omega the knife and told her to put it away—far away. I didn't ever want to see it again. Jay-Rod was still in too much of a shock to even speak.

·My blood finally started to circulate again Then I had a million questions to ask Omega. When had she seen them before? What happened then? How come she had three fingers? And on and on. Although Omega was a great one for asking questions, when it came to answering them, she was a bust. I could see it was going to take all of my digging to wheedle them out of her.

Meanwhile, Mom had driven our bus across the Taos mesa and up and over the Brazos Mountains. The scenery was spectacular, but our brains couldn't take it in at all. Jay-Rod still seemed to be in some sort of daze. "Wake up, little Bro! We're almost to the Apache Reservation. Maybe we'll see some Indians!" I waved my hand in front of his eyes as our bus pulled up to a gas station in Dulce. He came to with a start.

"No, Mom," were his first words. "We shouldn't be here! Let's turn around and go another way! Please, Mom. This is not the right road to take! Turn around!"

We were all startled by his frantic remarks. Mom just shook her head. There were no other roads through this mountainous country that would take us to Aztec. Mom pumped gas while Jay-Rod kept begging her to turn around. Omega and I went inside the convenience store to buy us some snacks. Yup, it was operated by Apache Indians and they were all the customers, too. It was cool to be in Indian country like this. Not for Jay-Rod, for some unknown reason.

Once back on the road Jay-Rod still refused to calm down. He was up in the front seat jumping around and arguing with Mom. She finally tried to hush him up by having him find our location on the map and be the navigator. Then he could see this was the only road.

"Tell us why, Bro," I asked him. "Why is this the wrong road? What's wrong with it? This Route 64 takes us right across the Apache Reservation and up to the turnoff to Aztec. You remember how much you wanted to see the ancient Indian Ruins at Aztec where Omega lives." That shut him up. Then he finally whispered: "It's the grays, Darry. They have a base here. There's an underground UFO base right here!"

Well, what could any of us say to that? Mom, of course, quickly entered the conversation. She wanted to know what in the world he meant by grays and UFOs. How did he know there was an underground base here? Why was he afraid about it?

That really blew our cover. I did not want Mom to get involved in any of this. The less she knew about our activities, the easier it was for us to carry them out. Not that she would really stop us. But maybe she would put the brakes on. I tried to tell her Jay-Rod had a bad dream about UFOs last night and was still thinking about it. That made more sense to her than all his mutterings about grays and an underground base.

Then I started reciting my latest chant. I make them up on the spot, you know, to get people's minds off negative things.

*UFOs, UFOs,*
*Who can tell us where they go?*
*In the sky, way up high,*
*We can see them all fly by. (Look up! Look up!)*

*UFOs, UFOs,*
*See them hiding down below,*
*Down-down-down, underground,*
*Hiding from us till they're found. (Look down! Look down!)*

*Deep-deep-deep, in our sleep,*
*It is just like counting sheep;*
*One-two-three-four-five-six-seven,*
*See them soaring up to heaven. (Gotcha!)*

Okay. So it's not Robert Frost. But everybody around here loves my rhymes, anyway. Yeah. If they don't, what can they do? So I decided, let's get this UFO business out of our system by saying it, chanting it, and repeating it, over and over until we're all sick of it. "Let's go again, everybody: UFOs, UFOs, etc, etc." Finally Omega whispered to me: "He's right, you know. There is a UFO base underground around Dulce."

Oh, man-o-man. What next?

What next was the town of Aztec itself. A sign on the road said: "Welcome to Aztec. Home of 6,283 Friendly People, and 6 Grouches." This was going to be fun. The Animas River ran right alongside the little town—between the town and the Aztec Ruins National Monument, the ancient Indian pueblo where Omega's father worked as a ranger. He called it the "Animal River" and asked us what kind of animals were we? Whoa!

There were no campgrounds close by, he told us. We should feel free to camp in his yard—if we would just put down clean straw on the ground and bring in our own fodder— feed, that is. If any of us were elephants there was a hose in back to wash us down! But he didn't want to hear any trumpeting or growling at night. And he didn't want to find any fresh coyote bones or magpie feathers in the morning!

Was her father one of them? The grouches, I mean? You gotta be kidding! He was the coolest, funniest Dad in the world. He was so glad to see his little girl and her two animal friends. (Us?) Or were we boyfriends? In that case, let's not have any love triangles at night!

I was shocked to find out he was an archaeologist, and with a PhD, too. Wow! I thought they were serious people. He said he was a "mav-er-ick," part **mas**todon (he was a big guy), part **var**icose veins (from leading so many guided tours), and part **ich**thyosaurus. I looked up "maverick" in Mom's dictionary (she is home-schooling Jay-Rod), and it gave meanings like "an unbranded animal," or "a person who acts on his independent beliefs." I loved the "unbranded animal" one.

But the trouble with a jokester is trying to get anything serious out of him. I never knew if he was giving us the straight scoop or putting us on. So we didn't find out much about petroglyphs from him. But then I happened to mention UFOs and it was like turning on a fast-breaking news broadcast from the History Channel. UFOs? UFOs were what made the Aztec town what it was today!!! Come again?

Didn't we know about the celebrated Aztec UFO crash in 1948? And the government cover-up? You gotta be kidding! It was even more famous than the Roswell crash ever thought of being! People all over the world came to Aztec to learn about it these days. There were tapes, a DVD, a huge book, and who knows what else more about it. Hadn't Omega even mentioned it? What was she thinking? She would have to take us out to Hart Canyon where it all happened and give us the scoop. He was on duty the next day so Omega would have to be our guide to a real UFO crash site. Whoa!

Mom stayed behind at the Ruins to paint, so I got to drive the bus again, with Omega in the front seat giving me directions. I didn't know what to expect. Maybe it was all one of her father's jokes, ya know. Jay-Rod was very nervous about it in case it had to do with gray ETs. (It did).

The site was about ten miles from Aztec over back roads—gravel, of course, and finally up a cut up the canyon road to the mesa top. A hand-painted sign stuck in a juniper tree pointed to "UFO" in that direction. We parked and walked in. Pinyon and juniper trees dotted the mesa till we came to a wide open space, about a hundred feet across.

This was it, claimed Omega. A big silver disk crash-landed here in 1948 with 12-to-14 ETs in it. None survived, but the disk did. It was practically undamaged. Next day the military swooped in. They bought up the land, brought in heavy equipment, and whisked the UFO and its dead occupants up to the Los Alamos atomic labs for testing.

There world-famous scientists (no longer alive) did their thing. Then the military threatened the land-owners, and any eye-witnesses that something terrible would happen to them if they so much as mentioned the UFO crash to anybody. It was a tight cover up—just like the government does today when people claim to see UFOs. The government still says they're seeing weather balloons or plane lights. Yup.

So how come people are talking about it now, more than sixty years after it happened, I wanted to know? Omega knew all about that, too. She told us UFO researchers recently found new files with military reports about it through the Freedom of Information Act. And finally the people who knew about it all along are beginning to open up. Elderly ranchers, military personnel, and eye-witnesses were giving death-bed confessions about it. It was a cold case that suddenly turned hot. Double-wow!

Jay-Rod looked sick. He wanted to go back to Aztec. But I wanted to know a lot more about it. Why did the disk crash? Omega said strong microwave radar beams probably made the disk lose power and crash. But why don't most people know about this, I kept wondering?

"They will," said Omega. "The whole terrible cover-up is about to come apart," she claimed. "Just wait. No more government secrets about anything, you'll see."

Did her father believe all this, I kept asking? Of course, but he worked for the National Park Service so he couldn't say more than he already had. Omega was his mouthpiece. Would our Mom believe this? Probably not—not just on Omega's say-so. She wasn't that much interested in UFOs, anyway. But I could see that Jay-Rod believed. And so did I—I guess.

Then Omega had this bright idea to prove a UFO had really been there. She got out the hunting knife (the one I never hoped to see again), and placed it on the ground—on "ground zero" she said, where the disk had landed. We stood back from it to see what would happen—in case it blew up or spouted sparks like a piece of fireworks on Fourth of July. Nothing! I thought so.

We went over to see if it was buzzing or anything. Nope. But then something did happen. The knife suddenly flipped over! Nobody touched it or anything. It just flipped all by itself. We all jumped back. Or did we imagine it?

"Don't pick it up yet," Omega warned. "Let's wait and see for a few minutes." Omygosh!

It did it again! That was enough for Jay-Rod. He ran back to the bus, hopped in, and slammed the door. I threw my jacket over it like it was alive, and carried the whole thing back out through the woods till we reached the bus. Then Omega put it inside her backpack still wrapped in my jacket.

I held the backpack up to my ear to see if I could hear anything. Yes. It was buzzing again! I felt sort of sick-to-my-stomach, myself. Did that mean Omega would be coming with us up to Utah? And we would be looking for the right petroglyph to tell us what to do next? Yikes!

Just like with the buzzing rock at Joshua Tree. I was in favor of tossing the whole thing out right there. But Omega wouldn't let me. She said as long as it was in her backpack, it was her property. And she thought it was valuable. But it was wrapped in my jacket, I reminded her. Okay, she told me, I could claim half of the reward. Reward? What reward? "Wait and see," she whispered mysteriously. Uuh!

# 4

# Newspaper Rock

Utah! Yippee! The land of the fabulous petroglyphs! We finally made it! I decided I was really gonna read the symbols in this Newspaper Rock we were now headed for. Maybe I could find out what we were suppose to do about our rock energy—or where we were supposed to go to find out what to do. Hah! I guess I was just like those early pioneers who thought the glyphs were picture writing you could read like a newspaper.

What a laugh! You'd know what I meant if you could only see that Newspaper Rock we visited in Indian Creek State Park off the road to Moab, Utah. The ancient "newspaper" was on the wall of a gigantic pink sandstone boulder, four stories high.

It looked like some prehistoric giant had taken a humongous bite out of the boulder, making a rock shelter. Then he painted the inside with black tar (desert varnish). Then every Indian who came along, had pecked out his own animal sign on the "blackboard." And if there wasn't room for his name, he pecked it on top of someone else's. Oh man-o-man! Maybe a thousand years of pecking!

There was Bernard Bear Paws, Simon Shooting Arrow, Sherman Deer Tracks, Eugene Hungry Wolfe, Victor Spotted Eagle, Joseph Buffalo Horns, Emerson Mountain Sheep, Harlan Halfmoon, Moses Long Neck, Basil Big Feet, and on and on. Ever hear of them? You know I'm just making up those names. But maybe not. Maybe some of those men really were the shamans who meditated in this sacred rock shelter over hundreds of years. Then added their visions to the "newspaper." Can't ya just see it?

Omega said there were three main groups of Indians who worshipped at Newspaper Rock. First came the Anasazi like the ones at Black Mesa, then the Fremonts (more on them later), and finally the Utes (modern Indians). Worshipped? I first thought the rock was supposed to be a newspaper. Nope. That was only the Anglo's idea. This place was like Black Mesa, a sacred site where shamans had visions. Uuh!

I finally found out where Omega gets all her information. From her father. Why not? He studied Indian petroglyphs all his life. I wish he'd've come along with us. No, said Jay-Rod. We need to figure this out for ourselves. What he would tell us would be an Anglo's interpretation.

And a joker's, I secretly added. He'd just as likely tell us that the horns on the heads of the anthro glyphs were antenna that tuned into the UFOs! Or that those big pink "footprints" on Newspaper Rock were really made by giants who could walk sideways up the cave wall! Pink? Oh, yeah. When you pecked through that dark varnish, the pink color of the rock underneath showed through.

Okay, then where does our information come form, I kept wondering? Hmm. From Mom, first off, then from the books we read, and finally from Jay-Rod's meditations and my "knowings." Those last two were the most important, according to Jay-Rod, because they were spiritual. Plus, events and things that just seem to happen "out of the blue."

Something like that did "just happen" when we first entered the park. We parked our bus and walked over to the short trail leading to Newspaper Rock. Mom went on down to the rock. Before we could go down, Jay-Rod and Omega spotted some Indian women with tables under brush shelters selling souvenirs. None of us had any money, of course, so we just ambled over to look at their beads, bracelets, and trinkets.

Then one of the women spied Omega's three-fingered hand, and started making a fuss about it. The other women got really excited, patting Omega's hand, smiling, and telling her something in their language, probably Ute. She nodded and smiled back at them. Finally the first woman pulled something out of a basket under her table, unwrapped it, and gave it to Omega.

"For you," she said. "You take. Find more."

What was it? Jay-Rod and me gathered round to see. It was a small dark greenish stone. It was sort of glittery and shaped almost like a heart, the size of a little potato chip. Omega thanked the woman. Then she asked:

"What kind of stone is this?"

The woman pointed up to the sky. She made her hand come down like a falling leaf. A stone falling out of the sky? Then she said something we couldn't understand. So Omega rewrapped the stone and put it in her backpack. Finally, we walked down the trail to see the petroglyphs.

Hundreds of glyphs were jumbled into a huge mass on the Rock. Some on top of others. It was nearly impossible to make sense out of any of them. A family of bighorn sheep. Circles, circles and more circles. A few ladders. Some big fat horned shamans. A man on horseback shooting a deer with a bow and arrow (definitely Ute). Many buffalos. More horned sheep. All kinds of curlicue lines. Lots of big footprints going up the wall. A line of tiny footprints next to the big ones. A big wagon wheel (medicine wheel?). One handprint outline. A path of deer tracks from the bottom to the top. Some snakes. A bug. Stalks of corn. A bulls eye. Men on horseback. A double circle with a cross inside. It was making me dizzy!

I didn't see any parrots like at Black Mesa, but there were plenty of chipped out holes, probably from gunshot. You know how "stupids" like to shoot at anything.

The glyphs were fenced off by a sturdy chain-link fence. You really couldn't get very close to them. But of course, this didn't stop Jay-Rod. He was over that fence like a deer vaulting a swimming pool. Mom had a fit. The few other tourists who were standing at the fence, started shouting at Jay-Rod.

"Get out of there, kid! This is a state park!"

Which he did, pretty quick. Then he started jumping up and down and shouting: "This is not a good place, Mom! The energy's not right. Let's go. C'mon Omega, Darry. Let's get out of here!" Hoo-boy!

Mom motioned for us to take him back to the bus. She wanted to take a few more pictures. Then she expected us to set up camp at the nearby campground. She tossed me the bus keys. She was going to be at the Rock for awhile shooting pictures and sketching. Then she would walk over to the campground.

What was the matter with Jay-Rod? The petroglyphs looked okay to me. Maybe a little over-done and jammed together. Jay-Rod had just not been the same since our run-in with the UFO. But it wasn't that. It was the petroglyphs themselves, he insisted. They were too crammed together to mean anything to anybody. And that made the energy so muddled up that it almost hurt to get close to them.

"Look at the Rock!" he told us, looking back toward the giant rock shelter. "See that beautiful pink boulder setting up against the pink cliffs. It is really something special. Then look at the huge opening into the rock. It's a holy place, all right, almost like a cathedral.

"It was holy for the shamans because it was a vortex—a portal into the spirit world. Then they spoiled it by putting so many different holy signs on the walls. Over hundreds and hundreds of years. Just think of all the different energies that gathered there. And then something happened. Some other kind of dark energy came in. That shut down the vortex. The Newspaper Rock portal is closed. The vortex is dead."

He heaved a big sigh, and then continued: "Some of those shamans really made the trip to another world when they did their trances inside that rock. And then they pecked out what happened on the walls when they came back. All that energy swirling around in there makes you dizzy. And the dark energy makes you sick. That's why it's not a good place."

Whew! That's the first time Omega heard Jay-Rod talk about some of the spiritual stuff he knew. What did she think about that? She sort of nodded, and then added something of her own.

"Yeah, Jay-Rod, I know what you mean. I didn't feel the same thing you did, though, down near the petroglyphs. But then I didn't jump the fence either and get so close to them. So it's your own fault.

"But if you want to see some great petroglyphs that aren't bunched together, then let's get going. Wait'll you see the other petroglyph sites in this canyon! It goes all the way over to Canyonlands National Park. I think you're really going to be surprised. Besides, I want to try to find another green stone like that Indian woman gave me. I have a feeling it's near some petroglyphs."

So off we went again in our orange camper bus. First to the campground and the spot

Mom already reserved. We put up our tent in a rush, and then left Mom a note. ("See ya later, alligator. We're off to hunt more petroglyphs. Bring you back a photo trophy!") Then on down the canyon road.

"Did you notice that some of those big footprints going up the wall at Newspaper Rock had six toes?" Omega wanted to know. "Do you think the ancient people really had six toes?"

"Like Ernest Hemingway's cats?" I couldn't help adding. "Who knows? There's all kinds of weird things around here," I noted, pointing to Jay-Rod. He stuck out his tongue at me.

"Seriously, Darry," she continued. "Do you think it's better to have more toes and fingers or less?"

Well, she had me there. I knew she was talking about her own hand. Hmm. So I told her: "I always say, 'the more, the merrier.' But when it comes to fingers or toes, I bet less is best. Think of it. Then you don't have so many nails to clip. And when you have to peck out your footprint on some stone wall, it won't take so long." She punched me in the stomach. (Not hard)

Her reply: "I said seriously, Darry. Can't you boys ever be serious about anything?"

I wanted to say, "just like your father," but decided that shutting up was better, if you know what I mean.

Then Omega went on very seriously herself.

"I heard what you said about the names of the shamans who pecked out their visions on Newspaper Rock. But you know, Darry, you got quite a few of them wrong. I think you overlooked some important shamans."

"Like who?" I grumbled, not liking to be corrected by a girl, and a little one, at that.

"Well, some of the ones I know are Winona Standing Bear, Eugenia Horned Sheep, Victoria Many Moons, Martha Turkey Feather, Esther Hummingbird, Joyce Straight Arrow, Lena Leaping Deer, Geraldine Running Rabbit, Alice Red Fox, Emma White Owl and June Coyote's Howl."

Whoa! What was she talking about? "Those are all women's names," I retorted. "I was talking about the shamans. You know, men."

"Who said shamans are men, Mr. Know-It-All?"

"Well, aren't they?"

"You kids think you know everything about Indians, but you don't have a father who's a professional Indian researcher. And who's part Cherokee Indian himself. He knew that many of the most important shamans were women. His own grandmother was one of them. That's my great-grandmother.

"The men got all the credit because they married women shamans and became their partners. That's what everyone wants to hear—that men are the medicine men, the big chiefs, the big deals. Especially white men."

Whoa! I wasn't sure I wanted to hear where this was going.

"Women make better shamans, anyway," she continued, "because they're more spiritual than men. I bet you didn't know that, did you? And they are the healers and caretakers of their people. So it makes more sense to have a woman shaman who can gather the proper medicine plants. Someone who can go into trances easier to find out what's wrong with a person, doesn't it? Yes. Women were the 'wise men' of many tribes, no matter what anyone says."

Well, you could have knocked me over with a parrot feather! Who knew? "But what about the petroglyphs? Don't they show mostly men," I wanted to know?

"That's only what you say. Look more closely," she said. "Most of the figures don't show which gender they are. So how do you know? You see what you look for. The stick figures and big anthros with horns could be women, not men, you know."

She also pointed out that the word "anthro-po-morph" means "human-like figure," not "man-like." Women shamans drew pictures of men on the rocks, too. They might not have wanted to draw a picture of themselves. Indian women don't like to call attention to themselves," she said. "But they certainly could peck out a picture of an Indian man on horseback shooting a deer with a bow-and-arrow. Or better yet, have one of their male assistants do the pecking."

Yep. I had to admit that was possible. That certainly made our quest for the right petroglyph to tell us what to do, a lot different. Or did it? What changed was our own ideas about shamans and petroglyphs. Would we be able to find any female glyphs? Did we need to? We hadn't really looked for them before.

You see what you look for, Omega said. We weren't looking for women, so we didn't see any. I wondered what else we had overlooked. One thing for sure: we needed to take Omega along with us. Also be sure to include her in our search. She knew more about petroglyphs than any of us, Mom included. I looked closely at Omega. Well, if her father really was part Cherokee, didn't that make Omega part Cherokee, too? She made a face at me.

"Do the math, baby!" she laughed.

Where was Jay-Rod in all this? I looked around. Well, where was he? We had stopped the bus to find a petroglyph site that Omega knew about. Jay-Rod must have slipped out of the bus and found the site on his own. I hoped so anyway. After all, it was my look-out to keep track of him.

We scrambled down stone steps to the bottom of the canyon. Then followed a trail across Indian Creek, and finally arrived at the site. There was Jay-Rod sitting with his legs crossed in front of a large block of stone with a figure pecked onto it. Oh-wow! It looked really prehistoric—like one of those huge elephant-type animals. You know, a mammoth!

Omega told us it was the famous Shay Canyon "mastodon." Someone had broken the stone block out of the cliff and hauled it away. But he was caught and made to return it. This so-called mastodon really looked like one except for the trunk part which was not very clear. She also said there was another better-looking "mastodon" with a raised trunk up the road at Moab.

Scientists knew that prehistoric man had hunted mastodons. But mastodons became extinct on this continent 10,000 years ago. So who made this petroglyph? It looked old, but no glyphs around here were that old, or were they?

Was it a hoax? Maybe, but maybe not, thought Omega. There were other things that scientists never considered. One was that prehistoric animals really did use this little canyon. In a dry streambed not too far away they even found the tracks in the rocks of a three-toed dinosaur. Whoa!

The other was that shamans in trance often saw not only the future but also the past. Historic shamans like the Anasazi could easily have seen one of those prehistoric animals as it lumbered by. When they came out of their trance, they might have pecked out their trance image of this gigantic animal. Scientists usually said it was native hunters who made the animal petroglyphs. Wrong. It was mostly shamans.

I told both Jarod and Omega that they could have been shamans themselves back in those days. I never would have included Omega before. Now I knew she was telling the truth about women shamans. What an awful thing we've done in our world—shut out women from all the important things that men do! I know they will get their power back someday soon. I just hope they won't use it against us stupid men! (But I didn't tell Omega!) I didn't have to. Little Omega came over and patted my back.

"It's all right, Darry. I appreciate what you're thinking. (Yikes, she could read my thoughts like Jay-Rod did!) "Don't worry, I will never use my power against any stupid man—most of the time! After all, I need you to drive the van. Also to help me find my green stones. I know they're valuable. Do you really think they came out of the sky?"

Before I could answer that, there was something else coming out of the sky—rain! What? It never rained here. Well, almost never. I knew that the shamans were the rainmakers of their people. This rain was starting to turn serious. No need to wait around to find out. We needed to get out of there before a flash flood decided to roar down this little canyon.

Back at the campground, Mom was fascinated with our petroglyph photos—especially of the mastodon. But it was Omega's green stone that really caught her eye. She was a rock hound herself, and knew right away what the glassy green stone was: a *moldavite*.

I never heard of moldavites before. Now we all gathered round the little green stone on the table in the camper bus. It was a raw, uncut stone, Mom said. If you held it up to the light you could see right through it. But in your hand it looked dark green, glassy, and rumply. While the rain came pounding down on the roof of our bus, Mom kept us spellbound with her story about it.

Moldavite, it seems, is considered to be a kind of *tektite*. Did you ever hear of those? Not me. Most tektites are small black stones that have come from outer space. I kid you not! Some scientists think they came from volcanic eruptions on the moon eons ago. Whoa! Others say maybe from meteorites or comets.

You find tektites scattered on the ground in certain places around the world like Australia and Southeast Asia, Mom told us. But almost all the moldavites in the world are found in only one place: The Czech Republic, around the Moldau River. True. Most scientists agree that they came from some kind of interplanetary collision. Enough heat had to be produced to melt the mineral into a glassy green stone.

Are they valuable? You bet. They've been used for jewelry, on precious religious objects, on sword handles, and on crowns and such. Stone Age people used them for cutting tools because they were so hard. (All this from rock-hound Mom)

But the most exciting thing of all about moldavites is their energy. You can actually feel the energy in a moldavite stone! Wow!

"New Age healers love to use moldavites to open people up," Mom claimed. (Now she sounds like Jay-Rod!)

We all had to handle Omega's stone to see what we could feel. Mom felt nothing. I sort of imagined I felt a tingle, but probably not. Omega said she felt a buzzing. (Oh, no, not another buzzing rock!) Jay-Rod got the most of all. He said the stone had a character all its own. Omega should keep it on her body. She should talk to it, and it would lead her to surprising places.

Where had the Indian woman got it from, we all wondered? Mom thought she either got it from a person who dropped it, or maybe from the rock shop in Moab.

"But the woman told Omega it came from the sky," I argued.

"Yes, someone probably told her that," Mom replied.

Was it possible she could have found it somewhere around here? After all, there were mastodons around here eons ago, and dinosaurs, too. Mom didn't think so. So the whole thing was both exciting and disappointing. We wanted to believe that the Indian woman had found the stone here, or seen it drop from the sky. We also wanted to know why the Indian woman had given it to Omega, in the first place.

After the rain let up and Mom had gone to bed, the three of us gathered down in the tent to discuss the matter further. Jay-Rod had more to say than he let on before.

"Show me your right hand, Omega," he said. "See? That's what the Indian woman saw. Your three fingers. That meant something important to her. It meant that you are a shaman. Yep. And the moldavite is a shaman's stone. So that means she is a shaman, too. I bet she was looking for a young female shaman to pass the stone along to. You were the one. She knew you would find out for yourself what to do with it when you came into your shaman powers."

Omygosh! Could that be true? Would an Indian shaman give a valuable stone like that to an Anglo she didn't even know? And a little kid, at that. Then I remembered after all, Omega was part Indian. Except for her white skin she looked like one. But I guess another shaman would know. Then Omega reminded us that the woman told her to find more. More moldavite stones?

"You better come into your powers pretty quick, Ms. Female Shaman," I told her, "if you're ever gonna figure this one out."

"It's 'we,' not 'me,' Mr. Know-It-All," she retorted. "You're the driver, remember."

Uhuh! All I could think to do was sing the *Paw Paw* song:

*Where, oh where, are the little green moldavites?*
*Where, oh where, are the little green moldavites?*
*Where, oh where, are the little green moldavites?*
*Way down yonder by the petroglyphs!*

# 5

# Vernal, Utah

Back at camp Mom had a map of Utah spread out on the bus table. She was drawing a sweeping yellow line with a highlighter up and over and up some more. I watched it nervously going up the highway to Moab, past Moab to I-70, west on I-70 to Highway 191, then up to… where in the cockeyed world? Vernal, Utah. Hoo-boy!

"Mom? What's the scoop? You playing tic-tac-toe on our one-and-only map of Utah?" All three of us hunched over her shoulder trying to figure out what the yellow line meant. All three of us knew that Moab with its exciting petroglyphs was a couldn't-wait destination next on our list of stops.

"Now, boys…oh yes, and girl, don't be alarmed. We have plenty of time. We'll all get to see everything we planned on seeing. Just hang tight for a minute."

By now Jarod was bouncing up and down, shaking the bus. I knew what was coming. He probably did too. Mom had met someone she just couldn't resist down at the Newspaper Rock. She was always meeting these people who loved her drawings and had just the opportunity she was waiting for. So drop everything and let's go!

Yup. That was it. This time it was some guy from Vernal, Utah. He claimed that the best petroglyphs in the world—bar none—she'd ever run into in her entire life were outside Vernal. Uuh! My heart sank lower than the Rio Grande gorge. What about the mastodon in Moab? And what about spectacular Arches National Park above the town? We all had read every brochure available and couldn't wait to get going to Moab.

Whoever heard of Vernal? I mean, come on! I could see it all now—some little godforsaken town in the middle of nowhere almost over to Colorado! So goodbye to red-rock Moab as we sped past the turnoff. Hello to I-70, thirty desolate miles ahead.

Well, I had to take back my feelings about I-70. Heading west we left the flat sagebrush country behind. Ahead was an entirely new and awesome world of redrock canyons. Its amazing views went on forever. There were even turnout overlooks where you could get out and gaze at the views. So of course we pulled off.

Mom seemed to be "transfixed" (Jarod's word) by the brilliant buttes and grandstand mountains. She quickly used up her camera battery and had to scrounge around in the bus for a second one while she recharged the first. Jarod was still hopping around. Now he hopped after Omega.

And Omega? She had discovered clusters of Indians sitting along the overlook edge. They had blankets spread out, selling souvenirs. Not just some cheap tomahawk knockoffs or headdresses made in China. These were real Indian crafts—silver and turquoise bracelets, rings, necklaces, and hand-made pottery. I could see that the women vendors had already spotted Omega's three-fingered hand. Of course they wanted to touch it. She just smiled and moved along.

Suddenly she planted herself in front of me with hands on hips, puffing out her chest.

"Well, do you notice anything?"

Say what? Oh. She was now wearing a necklace on a silver chain with a very familiar pendant hanging from it. It looked like Mom's Zuni ring, the amazing ring from our Joshua Tree adventures. Oh-wow!

"Omega, where did you get that? Looks like Mom's ring."

But I could see at a glance that nearby Mom was still wearing hers. Uh-huh. After recovering it from a sneaky cactus wren, I guess she learned her lesson and never took it off.

"It's my new Zuni necklace, silly boy. I traded it for the moldavite."

"You didn't! How could you, Omega? What a dumb thing to do!" That sent her into peels of laughter.

"Gotcha!" she giggled as she pulled the moldavite out of the little buckskin pouch she carried on a cord around her neck. "They liked my three fingers so well they gave it to me."

Wouldn't ya know it? Maybe Native Americans knew something about three-fingered hands that we didn't. Anyway, it sure made Omega proud to have one. The pedant itself had the same white, red, blue, and black triangles inlaid in a square face like Mom's ring, but they were arranged different. Beautiful.

Just like with Mom's ring, I got the distinct feeling Omega's pendant was some kind of map. I remembered how Mom's ring made a five-pointed star when you doubled its arrangement. And that star—when we drew it on our park map showed us where to bury Jarod's buzzing rock. (See our Joshua Tree book)

"Wow! That sure is cool, Omega. You better keep close track of it. So a hair-brained bird doesn't try to snatch it."

"You're the hair-brained one, Darrell, so keep your hands off it."

I let it drop, but now Jarod picked it up for a closer look. "Ostentatious!" he exclaimed. (His favorite word from Mark Twain's fool's gold story in the Joshua Tree book.) Jarod collected words like other people collect dollars.

Now Mom hustled us all back into the bus. We were off again. Past Green River, onto Highway 191. Then on up the long haul to Highway 40 over to Vernal. But Vernal was no dusty desert town. Surprise! It was a bustling city! Full of traffic, no place to park, and no motel rooms available anywhere. Whoa! New oil and gas drilling had made it a boom town. Lucky we were campers with no need for a room.

Mom got directions to the place where the man she met at Newspaper Rock lived. You know—the one who told her about the great petroglyphs at Vernal. She wasn't looking for a guided tour, only his directions to the petroglyphs and a campground. We stayed in the bus while she knocked on his door. She waited and waited and waited some more. Finally a man came to the door and produced a map. We weren't really paying much attention until Jarod started jumping up and down again, rocking the bus.

"Darry! Darry!" he mouthed without moving his lips. "That's the guy! It's him. Duck down! Don't let him see us!"

I grabbed the binoculars from the side door pocket and peered at him over the rim of the door. Omygosh! It was him! The same baddy who tried to steal Jay-Rod's hunting knife back at Petroglyph National Monument! Whoa! What did that mean?

"Don't tell Mom!" I hissed as I calmed down Jay-Rod. "Let's just act normal and see what he told her. Here she comes."

"Okay boys-and-girl, we're off to Rainbow Park campground on the Green River. The McKee Springs petroglyphs are located on the road to the camp. The McConkie Ranch group is further over from Vernal. We'll look for those when we finish with the Mckees. But first we need to get our campsite. Hang on, here we go again!"

Nothing about the man.

McKee-McConkie, McKee-McConkie. They sounded alike. A little bit conked out, if you asked me. Well, which road was it? First we tried one and then another. Neither seemed to take us where we wanted to go. Did that man give her bad directions? Finally Mom drove all the way back to the main road and started over again.

"Let Jay-Rod drive," was Omega's stupid suggestion since Jay-Rod was too young for a permit. (Although he knew how to drive. Don't tell Mom.)

"No. Darrell, it's your turn," said Mom.

Okay. Time for me to take charge and get this show on the right road. Off we bounced on a gravel road through dry desert country on one side and white volcanic rock dikes on the other. Up next was a sign reading: "Entering Dinosaur National Monument." Whoa! I slammed on the brakes.

"Mom! You never told us! This is a dinosaur park! "

"Now boys and girl, remember, we are up here to find petroglyphs, not dinosaurs. Yes, there is an old dinosaur quarry here, but it is closed. You used to be able to see it from an overlook. But the museum at the edge of the overlook is closed too. You can see all the dinosaur bones you want back at the Utah Field House of Natural History in Vernal. Let's keep going this way, Darrell. Come on."

I started up again, but with a crushed feeling. Who wanted to see dinosaur bones in an old museum? For me they needed to be out in the wild. Maybe I'd find one!

Now the road wound down into a brushy canyon with cliffs on one side to what we later learned was the McKee Spring Wash. Both Jay-Rod and Omega had their heads sticking out the windows in case a petroglyph should pop up. Not much chance. The canyon walls were too far away to make out any figures. Wrong.

"Stop! Stop! Stop!" screeched Jay-Rod.

I put on the brakes and pulled over. Nothing there. What did he see? A rattlesnake in the road? Naw. His imagination always spilled over the top. He whipped open the sliding side door and was out of the bus in a flash. Down the rocks he scrambled and up to... Omygosh! Petroglyphs! We all clambered down to take a look.

There they were, two huge anthro petroglyphs facing us, holding a diamond-shaped wand between them. Whoa! Look at them—pecked into a flat panel of rock facing us like a billboard.

"You're right!" exclaimed Jay-Rod. "It's an ancient billboard. It says, 'Welcome! This Is the Place!'"

Oh, c'mon! How could he tell that? You know Jay-Rod. He is in touch with all kinds of weird stuff nobody else can see or hear. But <u>what</u> petroglyphs! Enormous! Like nothing any of us had ever seen! All thoughts of dinosaurs flew out the window.

The largest anthro was about 3 ½ feet tall with a square hat on his head and hair hanging down to his shoulders. He stood inside a thick circle so you couldn't see his feet. His other hand held onto another large circle with circles inside it.

"Concentric," Mom called it.

"A shield," said Jay-Rod.

A smaller anthro had a mask over part of his head. A "bear mask" said Jay-Rod, pointing out another bear mask at the right. This smaller guy also wore ear bobs, a three-strand necklace, and maybe a little skirt. Was it a girl? Omega stuck out her tongue at me. On the right were the definite outlines of two buffaloes with humps and horns. Wow!

"You're calling those anthros guys again," Omega protested. "How do you know they're not a mother and daughter welcoming everybody to the big ceremony up ahead?"

Here we go again with all that stuff about female shamans. Now petroglyphs of females? Well, I guess from Omega's point of view they could be females. They sure didn't look threatening like warriors. Mom had a few things to tell us, too.

These are Fremont petroglyphs. They were named for the Fremont River down in Capitol Reef National Park where this type was first discovered, and where we would be going before long.

Yup, an entirely different breed of petroglyphs from the Anasazi ones we had seen before. Very old. Nobody knew where the Fremonts came from or what happened to them. But I could see that Jay-Rod did. He was shaking his head "yes" or nodding it "no" for every sentence Mom uttered.

Now he turned around and dashed back to the bus. I quickly fished out Mom's digital camera and snapped a few photos before we left.

If this was the welcoming committee, we needed to keep our eyes peeled for the ceremony up ahead as we drove along. Smooth, flat cliffs were best for petroglyphs. Those on the left seemed perfect but too far away to see any figures. I slowed down to look, but Mom kept urging me on.

"It's just a small campground, Darrell. We want to get there before all the sites are taken."

Well, where were the petroglyphs? They were supposed to be on the road to the campground. Here we were at the camp already. Jay-Rod claimed they were back on those far cliffs on the left. We should have stopped to find out. Mom said we'd stop there tomorrow.

Meanwhile, here was the campground with an empty site, just for us. A tent was on the site next door, but nobody around. What a place! It stood on the banks of the wide Green River which glided along past Split Mountain. Could a mountain be tipped over on its side? This one looked like it.

"Uplifted," said Mom.

Okay, but to me the mountain looked like a red and gray layer cake standing on its squished down side. And the Green River was really green! No wonder they called this place Rainbow Park. The whole area they called "land of the tilted rocks," added Mom. Uh-huh.

"Let's go back to the cliffs," begged Jay-Rod.

Mom ignored him, got her digital camera from me, and started printing off the Fremont pictures I just took. We all got copies. That shut up Jay-Rod and the rest of us, too. We just stared at the strange anthros. "Transfixed" described us perfectly.

Who in the whacko world were the Fremonts? Could these be the petroglyphs we were supposed to find? We needed to get Jay-Rod out there to talk to them. And what about some ceremony Omega said they were welcoming us to? After talking things over till the wee hours, we all three slept in the tent that night. Omega said she heard someone prowling around outside our tent. I slept like a fossilized dinosaur bone.

# 6

# Mckee Springs

After breakfast Mom set up her easel with the Fremont photos clipped to it for a morning of painting. That left us free to drive the bus back to the cliffs we wanted to see. "But no further, Darrell," she warned. She would keep in touch with her cell phone.

Back at the cliffs we pulled off the road into a roadside parking space. There was a trail up through rocks to the base of the cliffs. Oh, man-o-man! I could see figures in a row on the cliff face. They weren't little ones either. Jay-Rod scampered up ahead. He immediately seated himself at the feet of the largest figure.

Omygosh! What figures! They were huge—four or five feet tall. Pecked outlines of fantastic anthros with headdresses, necklaces, and earbobs. All stood in a row like a police lineup. Most held hands with each other or with a shield or with some strange looking pouch.

"This is it, Bro!" Jarod exclaimed. "These are the anthros we were supposed to find. They're going to tell us who they are and what we're supposed to do next."

Hoo-boy! How does he know these things? Meantime, Omega walked from one figure to another. Then she picked out her favorite and sat down in front of it. Me? I just wandered along the narrow path in front of the figures, in a daze.

One immense figure after another held the hand of the next figure—or else held onto… what? It looked like a pouch with a face on it. Could it be a…head? We're these people head-hunters? My stomach turned over.

But I started taking pictures anyway. Mom wanted as many as I could get of the best figures. Trouble was they were all "best." Jarod's figure was a big broad-shouldered guy with hair flat on top of his head. He had earbobs and two straps down his chest. One of his stick-figure arms held onto a "head" (?) pouch. The other held onto a spiral shield with sun-rays around it.

Holding onto the other side of the shield was a smaller filled-in figure. He had three feathers sticking up on his head and ear-bobs. He held a different-shaped pouch with his other hand. On the other side of the big guy a little figure held onto him with one arm. I took photos of all of them. Then Jay-Rod turned around and got up.

"How's this, Darry? It's a family scene with the father in front, the mother to one side, and a kid on the other. And that shield is a 'sun-shield' with a spiral for energy to come in."

I shook my head uncertainly. "Okay, if you say so, Bro. But what I want to know is who are they? What are they all doing here? Why are they all standing in a row like statues? Who was it all for? And what was it all for?"

His reply: "I'm getting the answers very slowly. I think if we do a ceremony with Omega's Zuni necklace the "thought bundles" I get could come through clearer. What I got so far tells me they came to help the Earth at a bad time in our prehistory. Like, they were bringing star energy from their planet to help planet Earth."

"Omygosh! Then they're extraterrestrials! Wow! And not the little grays."

"Right. They came to show the local Indians how to live...how to use the sun's rays to help them. Those pouches they're holding onto are very important. Something about why they came here. This so-called ceremony is their introduction to the natives. The natives were standing down below the cliff. Each of the Fremonts stood in front of their petroglyph picture and talked to the natives telepathically. The Fremonts had to stand up here and not get too close to the natives because of their strong vibrations." Whoa!

At that moment Omega hurried over to tell us we were about to have company. A blue Jeep Liberty SUV had pulled up next to our bus down below. I remembered seeing it at our campground. But where was its driver or occupants? We looked all over and waited for someone to appear. Nothing. Where could they be?

"Did you lock up, Darry?"

"Of course, not. Don't you remember, we were all so excited to get up to the cliffs we just took off." Uuh!

"Well, I guess we all better get down there fast."

All I could think of was the buzzing hunting knife in the poptop. "C.mon!" We skidded, and stumbled, and slid down that steep slope without even bothering about the path. But just as we got to the bottom, the jeep backed up and took off. It had tinted windows so we couldn't make out who was in it. Wouldn't ya know it? I quickly put up the poptop and hopped up into it.

"It's not here, Omega! The hunting knife is gone! The people in the jeep must have taken it!"

"You're not as smart as you think you are, Big Brother. Look!" She pulled the knife out from under her shirt. "Don't worry. I haven't let it out of my sight."

Jay-Rod took hold of the knife, turned it over, and then held it up to his ear? "I don't hear it buzzing, Omega. What's wrong with it?"

Omega had a real funny look on her face. "It was okay when I climbed up to the petroglyphs. But when I put it against one of the figures, it seemed to stop buzzing."

We all tried it again against our ears. Nope. Not a buzz in the bunch. Now she looked like she might cry.

"Never mind, Omega. Let's go back up there and you show us exactly what you did. This knife and that Joshua Tree buzzing rock of Jay-Rod's are mysteries to all of us. Maybe these Fremont figures can help us figure it all out. C'mon."

At first Omega couldn't remember which of the petroglyphs she had put the knife on. Did she actually touch them? No, she knew better than that. She had only held the knife blade as close to one as she dared. Which one?

Finally she chose the right one. It was a panel with a bunch of figures, circles, and swishes. It even had a little upside down guy. Whoa! It didn't look anything like the line-up of the first Fremont figures. These guys were not outlined like the others. They were all filled in. No faces or necklaces were visible. But they were holding onto things. It was probably done by a different artist, Omega thought. Fremonts had artists? Okay. But I liked the first bunch better.

The first guy on this panel was wearing a headdress with two big horns like a Viking. His left hand seemed to have five long needles sticking out (fingers?), but his right arm was attached to a large concentric-circle shield almost as big as him. Next came another filled-in guy almost touching that target-shield with his left arm. His right arm held one leg of the little upside down guy. A line attached that guy to another little circle shield. Other lines with circles went zigzagging off above his head.

"This is definitely the one, you guys," said Omega. "I tried to put the knife blade on the first figure. I couldn't. He was too high for me to reach. So I put it near his large circle shield.

That's when it happened. Suddenly the buzzing of the knife stopped. I was shocked! That's not what I meant to happen."

Put it back up there was my advice. She did, but nothing happened. She tried it again. Nothing. Then she tried putting the knife blade near the next guy. Nothing. Nothing on the little upside down guy either. So where did that leave us?

Then Jay-Rod spoke up. "You're supposed to try your necklace, Omega. Put the necklace pendant up to the big target-shield."

Yikes! She did and it nearly blew her away. Now the pendant was buzzing...just like the rock in Joshua Tree. What in the wacky universe was on that shield? We all held our hands over it. Nothing. We tried the knife blade near it again. Nothing. Omega wouldn't let us put the pendant near it again. I guess she was afraid it would lose its buzz like the knife had.

"Okay, Jay-Rod, what's with the shield?" I wanted to know. "How did you know Omega should put her pendant near it?" But Jay-Rod was playing coy. If he knew, he wasn't telling.

"Come on, Darry. There's nothing with the shield. Look at it. It's just a pecked-out circle on a rock."

I could see that. But this shield was bigger than the other ones—probably a couple of feet across. It was plain and not so fancy as some of the shields. The guy was plain, too, because he was all filled in. He was not an outline of a Fremont guy like the rest with all their trimmings.

Every single one of these Fremont anthros was of a different character, I now noticed. Not one of them alike. You could tell their differences by the necklaces they wore—or by their headdresses, or their earbobs, or their belts, or even their size. It suddenly came to me that they were real people. That's it! The Fremont petroglyphs were pictures of real people! From another planet! Here to help the Earth! Oh-wow!

"Okay. You tell us, Omega. You're the one who put the knife near that shield. Why did you choose that one?"

Omega couldn't seem to make up her mind whether to tell us or not. Maybe we would laugh at her. Finally she said: "I could feel it drawing me. It was pulling me to touch it with the knife. So I did, and the knife stopped buzzing."

I held my hand near the big shield. It sure wasn't drawing me. I held it near the little shield. Nope. Jay-Rod could barely reach it. Nothing. How could a pecked out picture on a stone do anything?

"Lift me up, Bro," Jay-Rod directed, and I hoisted him up to the big shield. He cocked his head and listened. "Yep. I hear it. A real low buzzing, almost like a growl."

I tried it too, but heard nothing. Omega wouldn't get near it. Hmmm. This was getting curious-er and curious-er, as Alice-in-Wonderland would remark.

Now Jay-Rod spread his arms out like wings. He started skipping down the path in front of the petroglyphs like a kid without a care in the world. He would stop in front of one Fremont guy. Then twirl around like he did to the Joshua trees, and then continue skipping and twirling all the way to the end. That path was rough and rocky. I hoped he wouldn't trip and break his neck. No such luck. (Just kidding).

When he came skipping back I grabbed him as he went by. "What's with the helicopter bit, Bro? You look like you're getting ready for a take off."

"You got it, Darry. This is a place where the Fremonts went up to their space ships. They could levitate! Maybe I can, too, if I can just get up my power. Let go, and let me give it another try."

"Oh, no you don't. Mom put me in charge of you. I can just see you sailing off into the wild blue yonder—leaving me behind waving a sorrowful so-long." That stopped him short. One thing about Jay-Rod was that once you got his attention, he pretty much went along with what you wanted. "So slow down!"

Okay. This time he started plodding down the path. He held his arms stretched out in front of him like a sleep-walker in a monster film. To understand what happened next you need to get an idea of what the cliff face looked like.

It wasn't all as smooth as a chalk board. There were vertical splits every few yards from the flat top of the canyon. The entire cliff was cracked apart from top to bottom. The petroglyphs were pecked onto the flat reddish surface of the rock faces between the cracks. Now

Jay-Rod turned his sleep-walking arms and pointed them at every crack in the canyon wall as he walked along.

Whoops! He stopped at one large crack and climbed into it. Oh, no! I rushed over to where he had disappeared. Too late!

"Jay-Rod? Where'd you go? Come back!" He was definitely a kid who needed a leash when he was on-the-loose. As I climbed after him I felt a strong gust of cool air sucking me into the crack.

"Jay-Rod!"

No sign of him. Although it was narrow, the crack seemed to go all the way through the cliff. But soon it got too narrow for me to squeeze through. Now Omega climbed up and tried squeezing through the crack. She didn't get far either. Both of us could see all the way out to the light at the other end of the crack. But no sign of Jay-Rod. Yikes!

"It's a portal," she announced. "A place where the Fremonts came in and went out."

Omygosh! Now what do we do? The cliff itself seemed to be cracked from its mesa top to its bottom. Maybe if we climbed up to the top of the cliff and followed the crack across the top, we could find him.

"Or how about using your cell phone?" Omega reminded me.

Why not? That's the first good idea to come out of her. At least she was not the kind of indigo kid who rushes into everything head first. I tried his cell phone and it rang, and rang, and rang. No answer. At least he had it turned on. I tried it again. He had it clipped to his belt, so he wouldn't lose it. It flashed and vibrated when it rang. He should have noticed. Nothing.

"Let's throw rocks into the crack. Maybe he'll hear them and come back." We threw and threw, and yelled and yelled. No Jay-Rod. "Let's go back and get your Mom, Darrell," whined Omega.

Nope. I was not leaving this spot until I found my brother. Besides, involving Mom would mess up everything. She would call in the fire department, the park police, the helicopter pilots, and probably the Marines. Then we would be forbidden forever to go off in the bus or anywhere near any petroglyphs ever again.

Jay-Rod was not afraid of anything, I knew that for a fact. Not that he was courageous or anything like that. He just didn't seem to know enough to be afraid of anything. Or else he felt he was protected from bad stuff. Whatever. So far it had worked. So now we had to contact him. Any more ideas?

"Well, long ago the Indians used smoke signals."

Good idea. So we tried that. There was plenty of dried brush and sticks around. We made a little fire in front of the crack and I used my jacket (I had retrieved it from Omega's backpack) to direct smoke billows into the opening. "That should smoke him out."

That smoke smelled pretty good. Omega said it was because what we were burning was sagebrush. You know, the kind they used for ceremonies. I thought I felt a movement behind me, and whipped around. Whoa! I was face-to-face with a big Fremont! Uh! I stepped backwards and nearly fell off the cliff! Oh! It was just a petroglyph on the wall at the crack opening. Whew! But I stared at him closely to see if he really could have moved.

"Omega, put your buzzing necklace pendant near this guy's head. I'll lift you up."

She couldn't quite reach his head. So she put the pendant near the anthro's necklace of eight round balls. I could swear his necklace lit up like a ringing cell phone. Maybe it was just the sun suddenly shining on that part of the canyon. But then we definitely heard a rustle from inside the cracked wall. And out stepped Jay-Rod! Whoa!

"Hey, you guys, what are you doing? Having a marshmallow roast without me?"

Where had he been? He was not telling. But he had a lot of other things to tell us. He was in contact with the Fremonts! Yup. They were not bad people at all. Head-hunters? Never. Not even warriors. The pouches they carried were for something very special. They were for rocks used for dowsing!! That's right. They used them to dowse to find water and minerals. And that's one of the big reasons they came to this planet in the first place.

They were after precious metals: gold, silver, copper, zinc, manganese, uranium, and others Jay-Rod had never heard of before. And also water. They carried a special rock in each of their pouches to use as a dowser. Different ones for different minerals. Like a metal detector.

The information they turned up was recorded. Not in writing. Electronically. In the shields, necklaces, headdresses and other ornaments they wore. I kid you not! They might look like simple natives with interesting headdresses, but that was just a disguise. The Fremonts were a high-tech race of people with high-powered equipment. They camouflaged it with Indian costume cover-ups! Oh-wow!

Eureka! Now I finally got it! Jay-Rod's buzzing rock from Joshua Tree National Park was a dowsing stone! Right on! It attracted certain metals and made them buzz. Right on! And the people who chased us at Joshua Tree and also the man at Petroglyph National Monument and Vernal were trying to get one of those dowsers so they could find the metals for themselves. Like gold. Double right on!

Now that the hunting knife had lost its power, Omega's necklace was the only dowser we had. Yes. She decided to wear it around her neck but keep it inside her shirt like she did the moldavite in its little pouch

Did the buzzing bother her? Not at all, she claimed. Maybe we should all make us one of those cool head-hunter bags like the Fremonts carried. That would be pretty neat, I figured. After all, weren't we Mighty Spiritual Beings too? Jay-Rod just rolled his eyes.

So where did we go from there? No sooner had we climbed down to the bus, than Mom appeared. She came walking up the road with a sketch pad under her arm. She was coming up from the welcoming petroglyph at the entrance to the canyon. How did she get down there?

Wouldn't ya know it, the man in the blue jeep SUV had given her a lift. Yes, they had stopped by our bus at first, but she didn't want to bother us. So she asked him to drop her off down the canyon. Now, if we didn't mind, she'd like a tour of our petroglyphs up on the cliff above.

So up we went again. I knew she would be just as wowed as we were by those huge "stylized figures."(artist talk). Yup. She just stood there in a daze. I carried up her easel while Jay-Rod brought her paints. She was soon all set to spend the rest of the day painting our super Mckee Springs anthros. We didn't breathe a word about our adventures. Would she believe us? Who knows?

Meanwhile, Jay-Rod was half-way along the path to the crack, and I sped after him. "Whoa, boy! Where ya going?" I couldn't believe he would try climbing into that crack again. That was exactly where he was heading. When he came to the opening, he suddenly plopped himself down in front of the Fremont figure. The one I thought had moved. Now what?

"He's the Guardian of the Gate, they told me, Darry. The Gate is that crack that takes you to another dimension."

"You didn't go to another dimension, did you, Jay-Rod?" I knew he wouldn't tell me. He just kept on talking about the Guardian.

"See that half circle line across his middle and out both sides? That's his rainbow. The rainbow is very important to the Fremonts. If you stand under the arch of a rainbow, it takes you to another dimension, Darry. Isn't that cool? Stone arches are just as important. That's why they liked this area so much. There's arches everywhere—in case you didn't notice. "

"That's crazy, Jay-Rod. How can you even get under the arch of any rainbow? If you try to go near one, it just gets further away. And anyway, how can you hear what he's saying? A picture on a rock, talking? You've lost your marbles." But then I remembered how Jay-Rod talked with the rocks at Joshua Tree Park.

"What else did he say?"

"We need to find 'Center Earth.' It's very important. And we should follow the rainbow to find it. He keeps saying that over and over."

"Follow the rainbow? Does he think we're Dorothy and he's the Wizard of Oz? What a wacko idea. And Center Earth? C'mon. What's that? The center of the Earth? Another wacko idea! Even if we could find it, why would we want to?"

Jay-Rod scrunched up his face at me.

"I thought we were on a mission to help the Earth, Darry. And we were supposed to find the right petroglyph that would tell us more. Well, isn't this one good enough?"

Whoa! He had me there. You know it. So where was Omega when we needed her? Maybe her peppy pendant could shed some sunlight on the whole hair-brained affair.

Wouldn't ya know it. She'd gone back to the panel with the little guy with the big target shield. The one that had disconnected her buzzing knife.

"Hey, Omega. What's the scoop? I thought you were staying away from that big target-shield like it would bite you."

"You guys! You guys! Have I got news! I know where we're supposed to go! I know what we're supposed to do! My necklace is not a dowser like your old hunting knife. It's the same as their necklaces. It's a communication device! It can talk, just like theirs do! Come on, I'll show you!." Now she ran up to one glyph after another and held her pendant up to each necklace. Nothing.

"See, what did I tell you? Isn't that wild? They're all saying the same thing."

I looked at Jay-Rod and he looked at me. We both shook our heads. If she heard their necklaces speaking it must be in some unknown language—like "mute."

"Well, didn't you hear them?" She took off her necklace and put it around my neck. "Put the pendant up to your ear."

Oh-wow! I didn't have to. It was coming through loud and clear—a telepathic message! No out-loud sound at all. But very clear inside my head. So now I rushed around to every anthro with a necklace and put the pendant up to it. I could reach up higher than Omega. She was right. They all said the same message inside my head:

"Follow the rainbow! Find Center Earth! Follow the rainbow! Find Center Earth". Omygosh!

When Jay-Rod heard the same thing he yelled, "Yippee! Let's go! Start up the Roadrunner (our bus)! Get Mom. Time's a-wasting! Let's follow the rainbow and find Center Earth!"

And then, you know what I added—to the tune from "The Wizard of Oz."

*We're off to find the Center,*
*The Center of Old Mother Earth!*
*We'll ride, and ride, and ride, and ride*
*In our orange Roadrunner bus;*
*A weird buzzing necklace and us!*

# 7

# Cell Phones

Back at the Rainbow Park campground, we gathered inside the tent to map out our next move. First we decided to put together everything each of us knew about these strange Fremont petroglyph figures. Good idea. I was appointed the recorder. Bad idea.

Me, a secretary? Omega should definitely be the secretary. She was the only girl. But I was out-voted—very loudly. I guessed that the Fremonts probably treated males and females as equals. Did we have to copy everything they did? Okay, okay, I would write down the info—if I could spell it.

What we know about the Fremonts (by Yours Truly):

> They were tall figures with broad shoulders.
> Their bodies slanted down to thin waists.
> Some had bucket-shaped heads with horns.
> Some wore headdresses.
> Some wore necklaces, breast plates, belts, or earbobs.
> Some carried pouches.
> Their pouches were not "trophy heads."
> Their pouches were for dowsing for water or minerals.
> They carried a dowsing rock in their pouches.
> They stood in a row on a cliff facing out (like a police lineup).
> They held each other's hands or their dowsing pouches.

Some held onto circular shields.

Their shields had strange electrical powers.

One shield stopped our hunting knife from buzzing.

It made Omega's pendant buzz.

The Fremonts were extraterrestrials (!)

They were a high tech race with high tech equipment.

The headdresses, necklaces, and things they wore were a disguise.

It covered up their high tech equipment.

They came to help the Earth.

They brought star energy from their planet.

They were not warriors.

Each figure was a different Fremont person.

Some panels showed a family scene with father, mother and child.

The Fremonts could levitate.

The Fremonts came to Earth inside a cliff opening at McKee Springs.

The opening was called The Gate to Another Dimension.

The rainbow was important to the Fremonts (also stone arches and stone bridges).

Omega's necklace was a communication device like their necklaces.

Their necklaces were all saying the same thing: "Follow the rainbow; Find Center Earth."

Yippee! I did it! (But don't tell Mom). Now everyone knew what we all knew. Whatever. But what did it all mean? Omega thought maybe the Fremonts were the original *kachinas*. You know—the kachinas that modern pueblo Indians still believed were holy beings, messengers to the gods. Certain chosen pueblo people still dressed in costumes like the kachinas and danced in ceremonial dances every year. Omega's father from Aztec, New Mexico told her all about them. Indian stores sold little imitation kachina dolls to tourists. Fremonts were kachinas? Maybe, I thought.

But then why don't the pueblo people today pay any attention to these Fremont petroglyphs? You would think they would be holding ceremonies here if the figures were important to them. No. They keep away from petroglyphs like they are bad medicine. Omega said all the modern Indians stay away from all the ancient ruins and petroglyphs because they still hold power. Rocks hold power?

"Don't you remember?" added Jay-Rod. "Indians believe that everything on Earth is alive: rocks, dirt, rain, clouds, wind, mountains, trees, plants, animals…everything. These rock pictures stand for real people who still have the powers the Fremonts did when they first came here. Sure the modern Indians stay away from them. I would too if I knew what their power could do to me. Look what it already did!"

One thing we knew for sure—we could tune into them by putting Omega's necklace up close to one of their necklaces. Their necklaces were like cell phones for them to communicate with each other. Now we were part of the loop. Was that good?

"They're just like our cell phones except you can't talk, only listen," declared Omega. "Or maybe you can talk. We just haven't learned how."

All this talk about cell phones, finally got to Jay-Rod. He groaned. We didn't pay any attention at first. He was always making funny noises. Then he groaned again. This time much louder. When we looked over at him, he looked like he might cry.

"Okay, Bro, out with it. Are you sick—or sending secret signals to the Fremonts—or just letting us know what you think of Omega's idea?"

He didn't answer. He just pointed to his belt where he kept his cell phone clipped. Oh-oh. No cell phone. Had he lost another one? He was always losing his cell phone. Mom was going to have a fit.

"But I had it when I went inside the crack in the cliff," he whined. "I know I did. I kept feeling for it as I went along in case something happened. When I came out again, I just popped out without any trouble. It must be back there. What am I going to do? Mom won't let me go out any more!"

"Never mind, Bro, we'll just go back and find it."

I knew Jay-Rod would have to do the squeezing through that narrow passage. None of us fit. Jay-Rod already claimed he didn't have to squeeze at all the first time. It was plenty wide. He never could understand why we didn't come all the way in after him. Now he would see.

When we finally got back to the path up to the McKee Springs petroglyphs, Jay-Rod was still whining about not wanting to go into the crack. But he would have to do it. We didn't fit. I kept telling him they wouldn't take him to another dimension this time, but he still acted scared.

We finally climbed up to the crack where the Guardian was pecked onto the wall. Guess what? It was all closed up! The crack, that is. Nobody could have squeezed into that passage now. It was jammed full of rocks from top to bottom. Hoo-boy! Where in the cockamany universe did they come from? Maybe there was a mini earthquake or something. We just stood and stared. The Guardian stared back at us.

"Put your necklace up to the Guardian's necklace and see what you get, Omega."

She did. No message this time.

"Hmmm. Some high tech necklace-phone! Lemme try it."

"Come in, Guardian of the Gate! Come in, Guardian of the Gate! Darrell calling. Where is Jay-Rod's cell phone! Over and out."

Nothing. None of us heard a single word of mental telepathy. What a phony phone!

"I don't think you're supposed to talk out loud, Darry," said Omega. "In mental telepathy you have to close your eyes and think the words over and over in your head instead of saying them."

"Okay. Let's do it."

So we closed our eyes and thought the words. All of a sudden we all heard a crackling sound in our heads. Like somebody had switched on the power. Then came a telepathic message saying: "Follow the rainbow. Follow the rainbow. Find center Earth. Find Center Earth. "

"Oh, man-o-man! Wouldn't ya know it? They've really got rainbows on the brain! Your cell phone is probably in the pot-of-gold at the end of the rainbow, Jay-Rod! Okay. Delete that. Don't get upset, Jay-Rod. I'll lend you my phone when you need to use one. But I guess we better get serious about this rainbow business."

"I think we should all go back to that big target-shield, the one that turned off Omega's buzzing knife." said Jay-Rod finally. "There is more to it than meets the eye."

That didn't surprise me even one smidgen. I knew Jay-Rod knew more about that shield than meets the tongue, too. His tongue, that is. When we finally stood in front of the weird panel with all its figures he closed his eyes.

"Now, don't go drifting off into dreamland without us, Jay-Rod."

"Shhhh! I'm meditating," he whispered.

I looked at the petroglyphs. Should you read this wacko panel from left to right like a newspaper? Or from right to left starting with the filled-in guy with the big horns that we talked about before? He held onto the big target-shield with one hand. Another filled-in guy held onto the far side of the shield with one of his hands. That guy's other hand held onto the little upside down guy. That one held onto a little target-shield. Can't you just see them all stretched out in a row holding onto each other for dear life like... Wait a minute! Now I got something, too.

If they didn't hold onto each other like that what would happen? They would all drift off into space! They were not heavy like us. Gravity didn't hold them down to Earth like it held us. They were like our astronauts on the moon. They were so full of ET energy that they weren't grounded. Whoa!

"You got it, Darry!" shouted Jay-Rod just like he was reading my mind.

Then he started telling us what else he heard from them. The first guy with big horns on his head was the Keeper of Energy for the Fremonts. He had to wear rubber boots up to his thighs while working on our planet to stay grounded. Whoa!

His big horns were antennas in contact with their Galactic Base Station. His name was Rakku. His target-shield was a huge energy monitor full of devices for recording information about the Earth. Each band of the target held certain kinds of information. Double-whoa!

But before Jay-Rod could utter another word my cell phone rang. It jolted us like an alarm clock waking us up from a dream. Was any of this real? The phone rang again. It was Mom back at our base camp telling us to come on back for lunch. Okay. At least I remembered to take a couple of pictures of the panel with Mom's digital. We would have to track down Jay-Rod's cell phone later.

Pot-of-gold—end of the rainbow—Fremont named Rakku—upside down guy. My head was spinning. Once back at camp Mom wanted to know if Jay-Rod's cell phone needed new batteries. She said when she called him, she got nothing but static. Then a strange voice came on that she couldn't understand.

"He was just fooling around as usual, Mom." I quickly replied making my voice sound low and grumbly like a monster's. "But fresh batteries would be a good idea." Whew! That was a close one! But who in the unicellular universe was talking on Jay-Rod's cell phone?

Mom finally printed off the pictures of the target-shield panel for us. Now we could really see the figures up close.

"Jay-Rod, what's with the little upside down guy? Is he dead or something? I remember reading that upside down anthro petroglyphs are thought by the scientists to represent dead people. Maybe he got electrocuted from all the energy! Did they tell you anything about him?"

Did they ever! They said he wasn't a real person at all but a symbol of the guy holding him. That guy came from a southern star where everything was upside down from us. He was what the big anthros called a "summer guy." The big anthros came from the North Star and were "winter guys." They were really all the same race, just from different stars.

Okay if you say so, Bro. But what about the little upside down animal under the summer guy's shield? The one with the pointed head, two legs, and a thick curled-down tail? Jay-Rod shook his head yes, but just couldn't bring himself to say what it was.

"Out with it, Jay-Rod. It's upside down like the little summer guy. So that must mean it came from the same southern star, too. Right? So what is it? His pet orangutan?"

Jay-Rod put his head down and whispered the muffled answer into his chest. "It's a d-d-d-dragon."

"What? A dragon? What kind of hair-brained stuff were they feeding you, Jay-Rod?" But once he managed to get out the word "dragon" he told us the rest.

Yes, they brought dragons with them for protection—like guard dogs. They called them *daracours*. They were large red animals with skin like an alligator and turquoise feathers around their necks and on the backs of their legs. Whoa! They were intelligent and peaceful. But they could be fierce if they needed to be. And they could communicate telepathically in words!

We both stood staring at Jay-Rod without a word. Dragons? Dragons? Dragons with feathers? I tried to imagine them, but I couldn't—at first. "Dragons aren't real, Jay-Rod. They're just a myth from a long time ago. Nobody believes they were real. Nobody even talks about dragons today."

"Except the Chinese," broke in Omega. "They celebrate New Years Day every year with dragon dances, you know. And Mexicans. The Aztecs and the Mayans and all. They carved stone "feathered serpents" on all their temples. They even called one of their ancient gods, the Feathered Serpent. Remember? But they really meant 'dragon.'"

Uhhh. How could I forget all those snake petroglyphs down at Albuquerque? But if this little petroglyph was an upside down picture of a dragon, why did they make it so small? I would think if they really had dragons they would make them stand out."

Jay-Rod shook his head vigorously. "They did. Darry. It's the swish. Look at the big double swish mark under the target-shield. It looks like a spinning fireworks pinwheel. See it? The swish stands for dragons, they told me." Then he muttered. "It's true, Darry. All this happened a long time ago. They said 1700 BC. That's almost four thousand years ago!"

Double-uhhh! I just swished my head back and forth. It was all too much. All these Fremont pictures on the rock walls. And nobody knew who put them there. Or what they meant. Or what happened to the Fremonts. Now dragons!

I was not going to believe any of it unless I had a real sign. Not just some imagined words in my head. It had to be something real I could hold onto with my hands. Like Jay-Rod's cell phone in a pot-of-gold, for instance! Oh-yeah!

But there was something we wouldn't be holding onto any more. Omega was starting to put stuff in her backpack for our trip with Mom over to the famous McConkie Ranch petroglyphs, when she gave a yelp.

"It's gone! I can't believe it's gone! You guys, the hunting knife is gone! I put it in my backpack after its buzzing stopped and I left it right here in the tent when we first came back. But see, it's not here any more." She dumped the contents on the tent floor. Somebody must have come in and taken it after we went back up there to look for Jay-Rod's cell phone."

Oh, man-o-man!

# 8

# McConkie Ranch

We turned the tent and its contents inside out. No knife. The hunting knife was definitely gone. We asked Mom about the knife. She didn't know what we were talking about. We also asked her about the man in Vernal who told her what petroglyphs she should see. Nothing. And what about whoever was driving the blue jeep? Well, yes. That man was the man from Vernal. Oh-wow!

He left after dropping her off back at the McKee petroglyphs. She hadn't seen him since. Just to change the subject: would she let us see any of her paintings. Nope. Not that either. We had to wait till she was finished.

So where did that leave us? At first we were laughing about the buzzless knife that someone had stolen—probably the man from Vernal. How long would it take him to find out he had a worthless blade? And then what would he do? Come after us again?

"You better hide that necklace in a safe place, Omega," warned Jay-Rod.

"You bet! It's right here around my neck—and under my shirt."

I looked at her quizzically and thought to myself: "The only way he could get that necklace, is to get Omega." Whoa! Not a happy thought. Mom didn't even believe the hunting knife was stolen. But she told Omega she would buy her a new one if it didn't turn up in a day or two. Yeah.

"Who's ready for McConkie's Ranch?"

That was Mom calling from the bus. We would still be camping at Rainbow Park. But she thought we better put our sleeping bags, clothes, and stuff in the back of the bus instead of leaving them in the tent—just to be on the safe side. Okay.

Everybody in the Rainbow Park campgrounds knew about the McConkie Ranch petroglyphs. In fact, all petroglyph lovers everywhere seemed to know about them. Mom had a book about them. We had even heard about them down at our Albuquerque camp.

"Don't miss seeing 'The Three Kings' and 'Bigfoot' at McConkie's Ranch," people told us. "They're hard to get to, but they make the petroglyphs around here (Albuquerque) look like chicken scratchngs!" Okay. But it was hard to believe they'd be better than the ones at McKee Springs.

Jay-Rod's excitement about these next petrogylphs was now like a balloon ready to pop as we drove down the road. He jumped up and down in the front seat. Finally Mom made him change seats with Omega and sit in back. Then he kept kicking her front seat. Mom pulled off the road and made him get into the wayback among our luggage.

"You're not going anywhere, young man, until you calm down!" she warned.

I was sitting in the back seat keeping my mouth shut and trying to tickle Jay every time he crawled up behind me. Finally, I had to join the fun too:

> McKee and McConkie,
> McKee and McConkie,
> Jay-Rod will ride on a
> Petroglyph donkey.
>
> When we arrive
> And he starts up the cliff
> Down he will fall
> When the poor donkey slips! (Hee-haw!)

We had to backtrack to Vernal and take another road out to Dry Fork Canyon. As we approached the ranch what first met our eyes was not petroglyphs. No-way! We couldn't keep our eyes off an amazing sight—hundreds of huge bleached elk antlers completely covered a long fence around the ranch!

Did that mean they shot all those elk? Nope. Mom said elk shed their antlers every year. Lots of ranchers pick up the antlers and hang them around their property. Awesome! I'm keeping my eyes open for a rack. (Didn't think I knew that term, did you?) What a neat trophy for my bedroom wall! The kids back home will think I shot it!

The ranch buildings were up as close to the pale canyon walls as they could get. The cliff walls were cracked and split like the walls at McKee Springs. They still had a lot of flat surfaces for petroglyphs. Most of the glyphs were high up on cliffs right behind the ranch building, people told us.

To get close to them you had to by-pass the fenced-in ranch on one of the long marked trails. These took you up to different levels on the cliffs. But to reach the topmost petroglyphs you had to be a fearless rock climber (Jay-Rod?).

We thought the McKee Springs petroglyphs were something special. Then we saw the McConkie petroglyphs. Hoo-ee! These took the whole tortilla! Panel after panel of lined-up Fremonts faced us with their arms stretched out. They too held hands with one another or with their dowsing pouches. Awesome! Some tall, some small, some with fancy headdresses, some with crying eyes. Oh-wow!

Where in the petrified universe should we start? Which ones should we talk to? Which ones were the key to the mystery of the Rainbow or Center Earth? It could take us a whole year to research this bunch!

Not for Jay-Rod. He zeroed in on one of the panels in a flash. Wouldn't ya know it? He got acquainted real quick with the figures on what I called "the skirt panel" (for the hula skirts). First came a guy with a square head, ear bobs, and a half-moon breast plate. Dots poured down from it almost to his belt. He held a long dotted stick or something in his own left hand. (A power-stick, said Jay-Rod,) with energy coming out the end of it.

His breast plate, belt, and earbobs kept him grounded on Earth, said Jay. He was a male engineer (!) who worked with water.

"See the large dowsing pouch he's holding onto with his right hand? It has a face painted on it with lines coming out of the eyes. Those stand for tears. The Fremonts used eye tears as their sign for water. (The "weeping-eye motif" Mom called it.). His dowsing pouch was for finding water—not a 'trophy head' like the scientists say."

Cool! Mom also says modern kachinas wear masks with "weeping eyes" like that. Whoa! So maybe the Fremonts really were the first kachinas.

All this took place four thousand years ago? Unbelievable! Jay-Rod said the guy's name was K-Barrab. What a neat name! I could see how the local people might make a kachina out of him.

"Oh, great K-Barrab! We salute you!" (Just kidding).

Jay-Rod scrunched up his face at me. I knew he was warning me to be more respectful. Okay. But what could K-Barrab, if there was such a person, do to me four thousand years later? I ask you. Ha!

But wait, the next petroglyph was bigger than the rest. He must have been wearing a mask because he had tear streaks coming from each eye—meaning he had something to do with water. Oh, yes. He was the Big Chihuahua controlling the entire Earth project! He even wore a crown. This Fremont's name was Vedor. Jay could feel his strong lion-type energy. Double hoo-boy!

This panel went on and on! How did Jay-Rod do it, tapping into such an important panel like that? And what were we to do with all these awesome facts? It was almost too much to take in. Omega said they never would have told Jay-Rod if they didn't want us to know it and use it. Hmmm. Well, should we all meditate? Listen to Omega's necklace? Or do a kachina dance? I couldn't see how any of this had anything to do with rainbows or Center Earth.

It had to do with water, Omega decided. The little water they got in this deserty place came mostly from rain. And rainbows only appeared when it rained—which rarely happened. Okay. Were we supposed to wait around here till it rained, hope for a rainbow, and then follow it? C'mon. We could turn into petroglyphs ourselves before that happened!

Then my cell phone rang. Wouldn't ya know it? It was Mom telling us to hurry on back to the bus. Something was wrong!

Oh, yeah. Something was wrong, all right. When Mom went back she found the side door of the bus wide open. Everything inside was now outside! Had we forgotten to lock it? Not this time. And what was someone looking for even in our clothes and sleeping bags? None of us ever left money or valuables inside, did we? Was anything missing? Mom had us check to see.

Uh-huh. Omega knew right away. Now her backpack was gone! None of us had taken any hiking gear with us except for water bottles. The trails to the petroglyphs were not that far from where we parked. But we all knew what the culprit was after—Omega's buzzing necklace. No use filling in Mom about that story.

We even knew who was after it—the baddie who took Jay-Rod's hunting knife at the Albuquerque park—and then took the same hunting knife out of Omega's pack back at Rainbow Park. That was the man Mom had talked to in Vernal. He had even given her a ride in his blue jeep SUV. We had his photo. Had she seen him again? Nope.

Just this morning we were laughing to think he had stolen an old hunting knife that no longer buzzed out of her pack. How long did it take him to find that out? What else was in her backpack? Just some baggies filled with stuff she needed. But he didn't know about the necklace—did he? How long before he would find that out?

When he did he would be after us again. Oh, yeah. We needed some kind of protection around the bus. Where was our swish? We needed a dragon to guard us! Our roadrunner decals on the doors weren't scaring off anybody. Maybe we could get Mom to paint us a couple of dragons.

How did he get into a locked bus, anyway? We didn't know. How did he even find us? That we could figure out. An orange camper bus like ours stood out like a forest fire in a snowfield. You know it!

Mom said she would think about painting dragons on the doors. I think she was tired of the roadrunner decals, anyway. Meanwhile, she printed off our photos of petroglyphs that Jay-Rod and me had been taking with her digital camera as we hiked along the first level of the cliffs.

Jay scrambled up higher and got more. But the top ones would take some acrobatic moves. If you finally got up to the highest level, the ledge was only six inches wide. No room to step back and take pictures of even one figure. And higher than that, there was no ledge at all. How did the Fremonts make their highest drawings?

"They levitated!" Omega reminded us.

Maybe we could tie a rope to Jay-Rod and lower him down from the top. He squelched that idea quick. How about hang-gliding? Can't you just see Jay-Rod gliding by and snapping a photo?

"You mean Darry," was his reply.

Then we found out that the Three Kings petroglyphs, (the best ones), were one of the highest of all. So we really put our minds to it. That meant meditating. So we did. That's when a funny thing happened. We all three got glimpses of the same thing: a circus parade! Whoa! Were we supposed to ride an elephant up the cliff? (Maybe a donkey!)

"C'mon, you guys, let's get serious. If the Fremonts could do it, so can we. Let's really think about what we saw in our circus parades. Okay?"

Clowns. (Jay Rod's answer). Horses and bare-back riders. (From me) And then Omega shouted out: "Stilt-walkers!" Yes. That was it. Why not? One of us could balance on stilts to take the pictures. Not me. Not Omega. Jay? No answer.

Then I remembered something about Jay-Rod, I haven't mentioned. Among his amazing indigo talents: he was a pole-climber. Yup. He could shinny up the slickest, highest pole you could imagine. Once he went up the flag pole at school and untangled the pulley rope at the top. Not stilts, but a pole was the thing. I figured that a ladder would be impossible to haul way up there through the rocks and trees. But a pole. You could slide it up from one level to the next. So we did.

I convinced Mom to let me drive back to town and get a long pole from the lumber yard I remembered seeing. Then the three of us pulled, pushed, and slid it up the cliff to the highest level. Omega and I braced it against a big rock. Then we held it steady while little Jay-Rod shinnied up that pole—just like raising the flag on Fourth of July! He got the pictures of the highest Fremonts. Then slid back down with a thump. Yippee!

When we got back to the parking place, there was Omega's backpack lying on the ground.

Whoa! Somebody had been there again and left it for her. But where did they come from? And where did they go? Three cars were parked next to our bus space just like before. Were they the same ones? Who knows?

We had seen other hikers and petroglyph seekers on the trails. Did that mean one of them had broken into our bus? Who knows? No use hiding somewhere to see if they would try it again. Where would we hide? Behind the elk antlers? Omega said they would not try the same thing again. She was sure. That meant we needed to figure out what their next move might be. She dumped out her returned pack to see if the thief left her other stuff. Yup. Several little baggies fell out.

"What's in 'em?" Curious me had to know.

"Oh, you know, tobacco, cornmeal, and stuff," she admitted.

"No, I don't know. What do you want tobacco for? Are you planning to roll your own?"

"They're for Indian ceremonies, silly. You know, for doing a ceremony when we approach some of the petroglyphs. My Dad gave them to me." Jay and me stood there with our mouths hanging open.

"Don't tell me you super petroglyph hunters never did a ceremony before."

Omega was serious. "You were the ones who were saying how sacred the petroglyph sites were. They are. And sometimes you have to do a little ceremony in order to get their permission to take pictures—or to get them to talk."

I couldn't believe it. Here this smart little girl and even her father were saying the petroglyphs were alive!

"Oh, Darrell, where do you think all this information comes from? These rocks were blessed by the Fremont artists. They have spirits in them. I guess they opened up to us without a ceremony because of the buzzing knife. But it won't always happen."

I shook my head. How could an educated park ranger believe such nonsense? Then I remembered his grandmother had been a Cherokee shaman. He was part Indian and so was Omega. Okay, okay. But how come Jay-Rod could get the petroglyphs to talk without a ceremony?

"He's an indigo with special powers, Darry. You know how wild animals come right up to him. The spirits of the petroglyphs opened up to him the same way." Jay-Rod was now making faces at me and clapping his hands. I could see it was going to be two against one unless I changed my ways. I might as well give in and try to go along with the program, weird as it was.

Meanwhile, Mom printed off our most recent photos for us and herself. She was all set to spend more time at the McConkie Ranch cliffs, but there was no campground nearby. So back to our tent at Rainbow Park we went. I copied down the license numbers of the cars at McConkie's before we left, just for good measure. But the blue Jeep Liberty was not among them.

The first photo Jay-Rod picked out showed just one big guy on a rock face. He had broad shoulders and a fancy breast plate. His arms were spread out wide but not holding anything. Instead he had hands—most of the Fremont glyphs so far didn't. And his hands were special. They had six fingers! That meant they were writer's fingers, said Jay-Rod. What? How does he know these things? I know, he always says that they tell him. Here we go again. So what was this guy writing?

He was the Head Record Keeper of this project. His headdress symbolized his position. It looked like two sticks standing straight up from his head, not horns, maybe feathers? "He used a metal stylus to write on metal plates," said Jay. "He wrote whatever they found from their dowsing."

Next to him was what they called a drill used to bring water up from underground. It seemed to be a small picture of a large object that looked like a $\underline{Y}$ standing on a flat line. That guy's name was Otul, pronounced "O'Toole." Think of that! Drilling for water four thousand years ago!

Then we came to the picture of Big Foot. Omygosh! You wouldn't believe it! What a wacko-looking guy. Like some kind of old time cartoon. No. I take it all back. He did not look anything like a cartoon—only his feet did.

He was a huge guy with not just lines for arms and legs like the other Fremonts. He and his body were drawn to look real with thick arms and legs. He was wearing a tunic, belted at the waist. His headdress was also different from all rest—tall and cone-shaped with a jewel in its middle. Straight horns (?) jutted out at an angle from either side like a Viking helmet.

His arms were opened with his hands up in a welcoming sign. He also had six fingers. His legs were short with knobby knees, and then came his feet—huge, fully-drawn bare feet with five toes. Hoo-boy! In his right hand he held a tall implement that looked like a monkey wrench (!). Behind his left shoulder a long, broad sword pointed down. Whatever artist pecked this picture was not the same as the one from McKee Springs, I'll say!

After I saw his photo I wanted to go right back there and see this guy for myself! I didn't care if I had to shinny up a pole to do it. Jay-Rod chuckled that he would be more than happy to hold the pole for me. Okay, so I let his pole jiggle a little, but I wouldn't have let him fall. Anyway, it would be worth it to see this petroglyph. Then Jay told us what it all meant.

Big Foot was a giant. There was not room on any cliff face to draw his complete figure, so they only drew his feet in their actual size. Whoa! His name was Rackurs. They wanted to show how big his feet were because when he walked he didn't leave just a footprint. He left an imprint on Earth! Yikes!

His sword was not that of a warrior, but a symbol of his power. It was pointed down like it was cutting into the ground because that's what he did. Made blueprints of different minerals and ores underground. He had x-ray vision and could see through the ground to where the minerals were located. Oh-wow!

What about "The Three Kings"? That was the next photo.

"That's a strange one, Darry. One of the three kings is not a king at all, but a robot!" What? "Yep. Look at the guy on the left side of the big king. He's smaller than the others and looks like he's floating. He's been pecked out—what Mom calls "in relief." All the rock around him is gone. He doesn't have any necklace or breast plate. Not even earbobs. Instead, those are controls on the front of his body. He's a robot!"

Whoa! I don't know where any of this was taking us, but I just had to know more.

"Did you get anything on the big king, at all, Jay-Rod?"

"I'll say. Look at his fancy shield. You won't see anything like that anywhere else in petroglyphs. I bet the local Indians got the idea for their shields from that one. Funny thing about it—it's not a shield at all. Not for protection. It's a disguise to cover his electronic message board. Yep. It sends and receives messages and signals.

His fancy necklace and breast plate are also transmitters and receptors. Even his crown is a part of it. And look at the row of dots coming down from each shoulder to his belt. They're all a disguise to cover up the electronic gear he uses as a *levitator*. Levitators raise the ore up into their space ships. Pretty cool, wouldn't you say?"

"I get it. He just has to click one of those buttons on his shirt and another load of gold or silver ore would go floating up to a waiting space ship. Yeah. That is pretty cool. You know, don't you, Jay. Nobody in the whole wacko world will believe any of this (including me). They'll say we made it all up."

"Let them. They've already got it all wrong, saying Fremont pouches were trophy heads. But think about us. We've been looking at the most amazing rock art in the entire world! We know who made it and what it's for. And we're part of their story now."

"Right on, little Bro. Ostentatious!"

# 9

# Fremont Indian Park

We spent most of the evening trying to figure out what "follow the rainbow" meant, and how we could do it. If we didn't follow the rainbow we wouldn't find Center Earth. If we didn't find Center Earth we wouldn't be able to help the Earth during the shift to come. Little did we know that most early pueblo tribes in North America had that for their goal, too—to find Center Earth. Yup.

Who gave them that goal, I wanted to know? Was it the Fremonts? For hundreds of years tribes migrated. Whole clans and villages at a time, according to Omega's father. They just abandoned their houses and kept going. Can't ya just see it? Some of the Indian ruins and cliff dwellings you see today are their abandoned villages.

How did they know where to go? Jay was always telling us how their leaders were shamans who were in touch with the spirits. The spirits would tell them it was time to leave. So they packed up and left. They left their marks wherever they traveled.

"Marks? What marks?" was my next question.

Petroglyphs! Wouldn't ya know it? All through Utah you can see their marks. The clans who followed the Fremont spirits made Fremont petroglyphs—hundreds of years after the real Fremonts had left the Earth.

Some of Mom's petroglyph books even had pictures labeled "Fremont." But they sure didn't look like the Fremont glyphs around here. Sure, they showed broad-shouldered guys with earbobs. Some even had "head-hunter" pouches. That meant they were still dowsing for water and minerals. But they were not the life-size Fremont guys we knew about, standing proudly in a row. Not "majestic," said Jay-Rod.

"That's because their petroglyphs were not made by the original Fremont people," said Jay-Rod. "Those people were long gone. They taught the local Indians all they needed to know. Then they packed up their minerals, levitated to their space ships, and took off. But they insisted the local people should find Center Earth just like they did. That was the only way to keep the Earth in balance," continued Jay.

"So, did the people find it?" That was my big question. "And if they did, how did they know they had found it?" My little question.

Mom had books about the pueblo people's migrations. After the Spanish came and then the Americans, most of the Indians stopped migrating. "But how did they know where to go in the first place?" You know me—always asking questions!

Omega said they went where they found water. If they found a stream they followed it. But if it didn't lead to Center Earth, they would have to go on. This took hundreds of years.

I can see it all now: Here is this Indian clan trekking through the desert. Finally, after many months they come to a stream. So they build adobe or stone huts. They plant crops, make pottery, and weave cloth just like the Fremonts taught them. They hold ceremonies and dress up like Fremonts (kachinas).The next year they add another layer of rooms on top of the first ones. Their shamans were in still contact with the Fremonts.

They made petroglyphs to show what they got in their trances. That's where all these Fremont petroglyphs came from. You don't see any more pictures of the first big guys because they were long gone. This went on for hundreds of years. Then one fine day their shamans got a new message. Time to leave and keep on looking for Center Earth. So they packed up everything and left. Well?

Jay and Omega thought maybe I got some of it right.

"But where did the rainbow come in?" I wanted to know.

"There are lots of places in the Southwest named for the rainbow. We should find out about them," Omega suggested.

"What about Rainbow Bridge?" Jay-Rod spoke up.

Suddenly Omega really came to life. "Know why it's called Rainbow Bridge? I just remembered. It's a big stone arch. In the Hopi language arches are called rainbows! And Arches National Park is called 'the place of the rainbows.' Shouldn't we go there, too? Maybe one of them is Center Earth." she added.

Mom, who was listening to our discussion, chimed in. "You won't find many petroglyphs in Arches. Especially not the kind you find here. But if you want to follow the Fremont, we should all go down to Capitol Reef National Park. That's got arches—and big Fremont petroglyphs. I'd really like to paint them. If I remember correctly, the native people call it "land of the sleeping rainbow."

"Let's go!" yelled Jay-Rod.

So that's how we got on the road the next day heading south. But we didn't quite make it all the way to Capitol Reef National Park. Wouldn't ya know it? We finally made it over to I-70 but it was getting late in the day. So instead if turning off at Utah 24 and going straight to Capitol Reef, Mom had a better idea. "Let's go to Fremont Indian State Park. It's not that much out-of-the-way. It has lots of Fremont petroglyphs, so I've heard, and a fine museum."

Okay. She was driving, not me. We would postpone the stone rainbows for another day. If a blue jeep was following us to Capitol Reef, won't they be surprised!

As we got closer on I-70 to the turnoff for the Fremont Indian State Park, Jay-Rod got antsier and antsier. He just couldn't sit still. But this time it wasn't from excitement. It was something else.

"Mom," he whined. "I don't think we should go there. There's something wrong with the place, Mom. I'm getting a bad feeling about this."

When Jay-Rod gets a bad feeling you know he's right-on. I know it and Jay knows it. But sometimes Mom just ignores it.

"Let's stop at the turnoff and take a break," I suggested. We finally pulled over, but by then Jay-Rod said it was too late. He wanted us to keep going and not stop. "This isn't a good place to stop, Mom. Keep going."

So we did. He kept complaining and making his noises all the way into the park till we got to the Visitor Center. Mom went in to find out about campgrounds. When she came out she tossed us a guide booklet to the trails. "I think you should read this out loud for everyone, Darrell. The part about Trail 13. Maybe this is what was bothering Jay-Rod."

Oh, man-o-man! I could hardly believe what I read! Especially because it was written in an official Utah State Park publication. It was all about the *Hopi curse*! I kid you not! It seems that Clear Creek Canyon and all the land around it were considered sacred by the Paiute and Hopi Indians. They're full of Fremont petroglyphs. And you know petroglyph sites are sacred.

Some of the Clear Creek petroglyphs told stories of how the people emerged from the underworld. Also how life on Earth began. Not only the petroglyphs, but the rocks themselves were sacred. The most sacred one of all was Spider Woman Rock, named after the Hopi Earth goddess.

That rock stood on a ridge and was shaped like a spider with its head facing towards Clear Creek. Petroglyph panels at the base of the ridge told the Hopi legend of Spider Woman and her creation of the people on Earth. So of course that was the very ridge the Utah Department of Transportation (UDOT) decided to level for the construction of Interstate highway I-70 in 1983! Wouldn't ya know it?

A Hopi religious leader visited the site just as the leveling started, to make sure Spider Woman Rock would be preserved. He asked that the ridge and rock be saved because it recorded the Hopi creation legend. One of the UDOT archaeologists said she would try to stop the construction. But when the Hopi returned to where the rock had stood he saw it was already destroyed and hauled away.

"I know about that!" shouted out Omega, suddenly perking up. "My Dad was always telling us how government departments never took Indians seriously. They never believed what native people told them. He knew all about the Utah I-70 fiasco!"

"The what? Okay. It was a fiasco. Hoo-boy, was it ever! I bet the Utah highway people are never ever going to ignore the Indians again. And if you'll let me finish the story you'll know why, Omega."

"Oops, sorry."

"That's okay. When this Hopi saw what happened he put a curse on the Utah Department of Transportation through Spider Woman. And also through her daughter Salt Woman who controls the weather. Yep. So the rain started falling and falling and falling in dry Utah in 1983. Billies Mountain slid down, blocking Highway 50 and flooding the town of Thistle. Utah Lake rose and covered I-15 near Provo.

"The Great Salt Lake covered I-80 near Kennecott. On I-70 new bridges over Fish Creek and Shingle Creek never completely settled. Workmen said all the concrete poured after the curse seemed to crack in the pattern of a spider web! I kid you not!

"It's right here in this Freemont Indian Park museum trail guide Mom gave me. Can ya believe it? The Hopi guy then clipped out all the news articles about the problems and sent them to the Utah director of transportation to show what Spider Woman was doing.

"Guess what happened then? Believe it or not, in 1985 most of the land in Clear Creek Canyon was donated for this Fremont Indian State Park and Visitor Center! Yup. The first one of its kind. How about that? But the park people didn't want to build a visitor center on land the Hopis had cursed. So they consulted with Hopi and Paiute leaders. Then they built it here in safe Little Dog Canyon, instead. If ya don't believe me, read it in the museum trail guide."

"I knew it! I knew it!" shouted Jay-Rod. "That's the bad feeling I had when we drove down I-70. I could feel the Hopi curse. But it's okay here. So I guess we can stay—overnight at least."

"But Jay-Rod, if what you were feeling is true, then the curse was never lifted. It's still going on." I was beginning to feel nervous. If the Utah parks and transportation people believed old Indian legends—maybe we should take them more seriously, too. I knew Jay-Rod already did and Omega, too. But you know me—whatever.

Finally we drove over to the campground and set up our tent. Mom worked inside the bus on her drawings. She also expected to do some phoning to friends, but her cell phone wasn't working. The curse? Naw. Probably just out of range of the closest transmitting tower. She asked me to try my cell, and mine didn't work either!

Then I had this awesome idea. Would Jay-Rod's missing phone work? I punched in his number and waited. Omygosh! Static! It must have turned on wherever it was.

"Hello. Hello. Anybody there?"

I pressed the phone against my ear to see if I could pick up an answer. It sounded like a low voice grumbling words I couldn't understand.

"Grummbble, grummbble, grummbble."

"Darrell here. Who's this? Where are you? What's your name?"

"Grummbble, grummbble, grrrreate, K-k-k-K-Barrrrabbb!"

Omygosh! I kid you not! I nearly dropped my phone! Somebody was really speaking. Maybe those weren't the exact words, but it sounded like that. It really shook me right down to my big toe! Whoa!

Was somebody playing a joke? But if our phones weren't working, how could his phone turn on like that? I turned my phone off and quickly put it away without telling anybody. Whew!

Next morning we drove back over to the Visitor Center to see what the museum had to offer. As soon as we walked in the clerk at the front desk asked if we had possibly lost a cell phone. What? Yup. The night watchman heard a cell phone ring and ring. He finally traced it to one of the exhibits.

Guess where he found the phone? Inside a large Fremont cooking pot!!! Whoa! And guess what else? It was Jay-Rod's missing phone—missing ever since he went into that crack in the rock at McKee Springs! Unbelievable! How in the hair-brained universe did it get there? The clerk said the watchman picked it up out of the pot and answered it, but heard nothing but static.

I was getting goose-bumps. Jay-Rod was stupefied. And the clerk was giving him a lecture about not disturbing the precious artifacts in the exhibit like that. He was too dumbfounded to answer her. Mom didn't know what to say at first. Then she had the idea that it was all some kind of trick we were playing—that we had somehow sneaked into the museum and put the phone in the pot. When she said that, tears started trickling down Jay-Rod's face. Did she think he was lying about losing his phone? Jay-Rod never lied. Then she turned her dark looks on me. I didn't show any tears, but just shook my head, turned around, and walked out.

Once out in the bus, I suddenly knew how to resolve this weird turn of events. I handed Jay-Rod's phone to Mom and punched in his phone number on my phone. Surprise. His dead phone lit up and rang. She answered it and soon her face had a real strange look. "Here," she said to me, her voice shaking. "Listen, and see what you think."

Yep. I knew what she heard and what I was about to hear: "Gr-r-r-reat K-k-k-K- Barrrabb!" I passed the phone around so everybody got a chance to hear it. We explained to Mom that K-Barrab was one of the big Fremont petrogylph guys on the cliff at the McConkie Ranch.

He had told Jay-Rod telepathically he was an engineer who built pumps for the local people to get water to their fields. And I said how much I liked his name and that he would make a cool kachina. Now here he was on the other end of Jay-Rod's non-working cell phone!

Mom was flabbergasted. (Jay's word) This was just too much supernatural stuff for her to take in one day. First the Hopi curse. Then Jay's phone appearing like magic in an Indian pot. And now a strange Fremont guy from 4,000 years ago actually talking on a dead phone!

Us kids started whispering together about how this last thing could have happened. We knew the petroglyphs were images of real Fremont people. We also felt that somehow they put some of their spirit into the glyphs so they could talk. So were K-Barrab's phone words actually spoken out loud, or were they telephathic, I wanted to know.

Telephatic, we all decided. We heard them inside our heads and not outside on the phone. If we held the phone up, we heard nothing. We had to put the phone up against our ears to hear his name inside our heads. Those were the only words we heard. Maybe that meant K-Barrab put them in the phone at the time he got the phone from Jay-Rod back at McKee

Springs. We would have to check the phone from time to time to see if the message changed.

But for me, the cell phone in the pot was a huge enlightenment! Remember how I said I wanted some kind of physical proof of what the others were hearing? Something impossible like maybe Jay-Rod's missing phone turning up in the pot of gold at the end of the rainbow? Whoa! Could it be any more physical than this? And in a real Fremont pot? Hoo-boy! It raised the hair on my arms! Did that mean I finally believed all this weird stuff? Hmm. What more did I need for proof? This Fremont stuff was freaking us all out.

Mom wanted us to follow one of the self-guided trails. I couldn't keep my mind on the trail or the petroglyphs. I kept glancing back toward the parking lot every other minute to see if a blue jeep showed up, or if anybody tried to mess with our bus. So I let the others go on while I wandered on back to the Visitor Center.

Finally we hiked along Clear Creek and under a bridge at I-70 to the Cave of a Hundred Hands. Another strange thing had happened when the Utah Department of Transportation built this I-70 bridge over Clear Creek. Some of the swallows in the canyon abandoned their nests and built new nests on the steel girders under the bridge. I kid you not! A sign from Spider Woman that the bridge was safe, said Jay-Rod. Hoo-boy!

The cave was a natural overhang about 7 feet high and 10 feet deep. Thirty-one handprints were stamped on the inside rock wall by daubing red pigment on a hand and pressing it against the wall. Where did they get the name Cave of a *Hundred* Hands? Too lazy to count 'em? You know what Omega was looking for. And she actually found one—a three-fingered hand! (Or were the other two fingers too faint to see? I teased her). These pictographs were made by the Indians who lived nearby on Five Finger Ridge over a thousand years ago.

When we got back to our locked bus, the side door was standing open! Uuuh!

Now what was missing? Nothing we could put a finger on. But things were tossed around a bit. Somebody had been inside looking for something. We looked at Omega but she shook her head. The Zuni necklace was safely tucked inside her shirt and her moldavite stone was in its pouch.

After that none of us wanted to camp there another night. After all, what were we doing there? Mom didn't get to paint anything. The petroglyphs, except for the big guy were not the kind we were looking for. And if we were trying to avoid the blue jeep, forget that. We asked at the Visitor Center if they had seen a blue jeep today. One of the rangers said two blues and one red jeep had been there yesterday! Hoo-boy!.

Then we asked if they knew anything about arches or rainbows. They said to get on over to Trail 10, the Arch of Art, that some say is just like a stone rainbow! Whoa! We went over and viewed the arch on the canyon wall and saw how the curve of the rock made it look like a stone rainbow. Would the Fremonts have felt the same? There was no real arch to stand under and nothing about Center Earth.

Sixty-one petroglyph panels were visible in the canyon walls, they told us. We didn't count 'em. One was a Hopi initiation panel showing small Fremont figures. One had the hair style of a Hopi male as a child. Another showed the style young men wore. So were the Hopis of today taught by the Fremonts? Could be. Then two blue Jeep Libertys passed by! Believe it or not! Count 'em! So we got out of there fast.

# 10

# Capitol Reef National Park: Chimney Rock

I love it when we start out for unknown places. What're they gonna look like? What's gonna happen there? I remember how excited we were when Jay-Rod hopped out of our orange VW bus in Joshua Tree National Park and found that buzzing rock. And how "flabbergasted" we were down at the Albuquerque park when our hunting knife started buzzing. So now—what's gonna happen in Capitol Reef National Park?

I kept thinking it was spelled wrong. It should be "Capital" like our nation's capital in Washington, D.C. But, no. This "capitol" was like the *capitol building* in Washington. Come again? How could a national park be like a building? I soon found out. This park was full of capitol *domes!* That's right. They were all over the place! Gigantic rock formations that looked exactly like the rounded, pointed dome of our nation's Capitol building. Yup.

But what about the "reef" in the name? I thought reefs were underwater coral formations in the ocean. Right. But this reef was a long stone wall blockade, the Waterpocket Fold, (Don'tcha love the name!) running a hundred miles like a slash across Utah. The Fold was where the continent folded under the Rocky Mountains. Whoa! It sure was an amazing sight when we finally saw it from an overlook. The flat land was actually folded, but didn't break open.

Oh sure, there was a fault somewhere down under there. You know it! The National Park was created to protect this strange geologic feature. No supermarkets or high rises here evermore. So that was it. A long, narrow National Park that ran along the Waterpocket Fold. Can't ya just see it?

If you know me, I'm always wondering about things. Like—what would happen if the land just broke open instead of being folded? And suddenly it came to me!!! That's what this Center Earth thing is all about! If the continent did break open at the Fold, we would all be doomed, and the Earth, too. The Fremonts knew about this possibility all those thousands of years ago. So when they got here they had to find the spot—the exact center spot—and put their star energy into it to hold the Fold in place.

Eureka! That's it! I could feel the truth of it shivering up my body from my big toes clear up to the hair on my head!

The Fremonts first came in their spaceships up around Vernal more than four thousand years ago. They were attracted by the big animals (mastodons?) up there, said Jay-Rod. But they knew that wasn't Center Earth. So they had to do what we're doing—look for Center Earth. You know it! And they found it, I'm sure of it—right there where we're going—to Capitol Reef National Park! Whoopee! Of course, it wasn't a park then, and of course there weren't any roads. But they found it just the same!

Then what did they do? Hoo-boy! I'm not sure. Jay-Rod thinks they put their star energy into it. (Whatever that means). I think they also told all the native people they had to find the place, too. To keep the Earth balanced. There were no maps in those days. So the tribes had to follow the messages they got from the Fremonts to find Center Earth. And who is left on Earth to find Center Earth today? Uuuuuh! Us? Omygosh!

I almost swallowed my gum when I thought about it! Should I tell the others? You know I can't keep my mouth shut. And how in the hair-brained universe were we little Earthlings ever going to do such a thing? Balance the Earth? Why not jump over the moon on a cow's back, instead!

Everybody but Mom in our moving bus was busy sleeping by now. Or else dazed speechless by the wonderland of canyons they saw as we zipped along I-70. Anyway, nobody was saying anything. I could feel a song coming on, wouldn't ya know it? But I sang it under my breath to be safe.

*Here we go off to find Center Earth,*
*Find Center Earth, Find Center Earth,*
*Here we go off to find Center Earth,*
*Three Mighty Spiritual Beings.*

Okay, so it wasn't Mozart—just "Here We Go Round the Mulberry Bush" in Darrell-time. But our quest was almost as whacky as that one, if you ask me. So I got bolder and sang it out loud, adding a couple of verses.

*What will we do when we find Center Earth?*
and
*Find a big arch put our energy down.*

Soon everybody was joining in and clapping. The joint was rocking! Then Jay-Rod had to yell, "Stop, Mom! Stop the bus! Turn here!" He was our navigator and usually had a good reason for telling us which way to go. But this turn-off sure wasn't the right road to the park, was it? Mom pulled over to look at the map.

"I don't know, Jarod," she shook her head. "It doesn't look very promising."

"Yes, Mom, this is the right way. Let's go!"

So up the nearby mountain we went. Beautiful scenery. But we soon ran out of road. Pavement, that is. And on we went bouncing up gravel switchbacks to the top of the mountain. This was the way to Capitol Gorge? More like halfway to heaven! Then its location signs began to work on me: "Frying Pan Flat," "Last Chance Creek," "South Last Chance Creek." Hoo-boy! I wouldn't mind living there. (Just kidding).

It was very volcanic-y at the top. Mostly barren. Three volcanic peaks rose even higher than ours in the distance. We could trace an ancient lava flow with black boulders strewn everywhere. And you could see forever in all directions. Then a big black-and-white magpie flew up to greet us. Remote or not, we liked it. So we all got out and stretched. The magpie wanted to land on Jay's head but he shook it off.

"What a great way to enter into Capitol Reef National Park," I had to admit.

"Entries are important," I heard someone say. Who? It didn't come from any of us. What's going on here? Has K-Barrab suddenly taken up English?

I didn't see any blue jeeps around either, or any kind of anything, for that matter. Maybe Jay-Rod really had "shaken" our follower—or not. In fact, we were all by ourselves on the trip down the other side of the mountain—through the little Mormon towns of Fremont, Loa, and finally Torrey, closest to the park.

Suddenly we were there and into the park. No regular entrance gate or sign to tell us. But I knew we were in Capitol Reef National Park for the colors of the rocks. Back on the mountaintop it was all black and white. Down here it was long, brilliant layers of rock—brown at the bottom, then red, then green, then purple, then white, then lavender, with a pink "castle" on top. I kid you not! Mom said it again: "the canyon of the sleeping rainbow."

That was when I realized it wasn't a real rainbow or even an arch that marked Center Earth. It was the bands of rocks themselves—the rainbow of rocks! I was glad Mom was driving, so we all could gaze at the wonder of it. We kept pleading with her to stop here, Mom, stop there. But on she drove.

Mom wanted to keep going all the way through the Capitol Reef valley till we came to the campground. It was a first-come-first-served deal. We kids wanted to stop at every rock feature we passed, but she whisked us along. Then there were cars ahead of us moving too slow. So she finally pulled off at the tall red Chimney Rock. Every western park has one of these, she remarked. But I got a funny feeling about this one. We finally got out and walked around.

"It's not a chimney," whispered Jay-Rod. "It's a person."

"Oh, come on, Jay," I cracked. "What's his name?"

Jay-Rod stood statue-still with his eyes on the huge red pinnacle—600 feet tall, at least, plus a 60-foot tan-colored cap with white on top. "We need to talk to him, Darry."

"What? Climb all the way up those straight 600-foot sides? I'd rather send up a message tied to the leg of a magpie! Or better yet, we could heave your non-working cell phone up there. No? Too high? Well, we could always shoot it up with a slingshot! He'd love to hear from K-Barrab, I bet."

"Get serious, Darry! This is important!"

"Boys, there's a hiking trail that goes all the way around Chimney Rock in case you want to take it later. The rock itself is made of soft red Moenkopi sandstone with a cap of harder Shinarump rock that protects the column from erosion, according to my book," Mom read aloud. She always had tons of scientific stuff to tell us whether we wanted to know it or not. I sort of took a fancy to that Shinarump rock stuff. You know me.

Once we found the campground, we set up the tent to proclaim our site possession. Then Mom drove us back to the Visitor Center we had passed earlier. These National Park Visitor Centers are for me! They're great. Lots of books, tapes, DVDs, stuffed animals, tee shirts, and camping gear. Plus they show films of the park. This one also had a diorama of the park spread out on a long table—you know, a 3-D map of the whole place with tiny figures, trees, and stuff.

While the others were busy checking out souvenirs to buy, Omega whispered to me. "We need to drive back to Chimney Rock, Darry. Ask your mother for the bus keys."

Omega had been jumping around in the store, trying on hats, cuddling stuffed animal dolls, picking up everything that was loose, just like Jay-Rod. Mom tried to calm them both down by saying she would buy one souvenir for each of them. That just stirred them up more, grabbing each other's prizes. But then the music playing in the Center changed to an Indian flute number. Omega stopped in her tracks.

"That's *Spiritlands*!" she exclaimed. "My Dad's favorite! I've got to have it!" So Mom bought the CD for her. I liked the music, too. It sounded whispery and very Indian, with flute and drumbeats echoing against canyon cliffs. Mom also gave me the bus keys with strong instructions to be back in an hour. And don't go anywhere but Chimney Rock.

I slid Omega's CD in the player slot and started the bus. We were off again to the flute music of *Spiritlands* on the road to Center Earth! But when I started to turn off at Chimney Rock, Omega egged me on further up the road. Uuh!

"Darry, I've got a better idea of how we can talk to the spirit of Chimney Rock. Take the turnoff on the right up at Panorama Point. See it? It goes all the way up to the top of the cliff on the opposite side of the road. Okay? That should bring us almost across from the top of Chimney Rock."

She was right. Up we went. If we parked in the lot closest to the edge of the cliff, there was the back side of Chimney Rock right across the road from us. We couldn't see the whole Rock, top to bottom. But the upper half was clearly visible, including the Shinarump cap. Omygosh!

We all hopped out of the bus and stared. This side of the large square cap had a face! I kid you not! You could see eyes, a long vertical nose, and a mouth. The whole face seemed to be carved out naturally showing cheeks and a chin just like the stone faces on Easter Island! Hoo-boy!

By now Omega was sitting cross-legged on the ground doing a ceremony with tobacco and cornmeal. Flute music from the *Spiritlands* CD in the bus was playing in the background. Jay-Rod and I sank down on the ground beside her. It was a solemn moment. Then she started talking to us.

"We have awakened a sleeping giant, boys. He's awake because we acknowledged him. He says he is a Sentinel facing east toward the Waterpocket Fold. He is the male Keeper of Middle Earth which is female. The crack in the Earth at the Fold must be kept in check. The flute music we are playing wakes up the mountains. He loves it, too. The white on top of his head is secreted alkali. It makes him look distinguished. (I thought it was from pigeons!)

"We came into the park the way we did so we could meet and awaken him first," she continued. "Now we must go through the whole park. We must put our energy into other important rocks. Our energy is the heart energy you two carry from Heart Rock in Joshua Tree National Park, remember? But we must be careful with it. It may attract others. Now we should go."

Whew! I bowed goodbye to Mr. Shinarump, just like Omega did, and herded the others back into the bus. We would pick up Mom at the Visitor Center. Then head back to our camp to make our plans. Hoo-boy! Omega was sure something else! She was like Jarod with her ten-year-old liveliness. In the next breath, she could turn on her serious side and tune in to the spirit world. Me? I just went along for the ride.

Now what should we do? We had certainly accomplished part of our mission to find Center Earth and put the heart energy into part of it. But it sounded like more was expected of us. We had to put the energy into other important rocks. What were they? Mr.Shinarump didn't say. Would the Fremont petroglyphs here that Mom talked about help us?

Before we could decide on anything Mom came back from the restroom with news. There was a blue Jeep Liberty parked at a site way over on the far side of the campground! She knew we were trying to stay away from blue jeeps but she didn't know why. She never pried into our private affairs. What a cool Mom! But what a nasty turn of events.

Omega said she'd sneak over there and get their license number. Then we could compare it with the one I got from Rainbow Park. Then we'd know for sure if it belonged to the baddies who were following us.

I thought we really should send Mom. She was still friends with the man from Vernal who drove a Liberty jeep. But Omega took off before we could stop her. So we waited for her to come back. And waited. And waited. Jay-Rod decided to go look for her. I went along this time. No use having him disappear, too. We were real sneaky. We stayed a long way from the jeep, using binoculars to read the license plate! It was the same!!! Uuuh!

Where was Omega? That really had us worried. Maybe she met some kids at one of the other camp sites. We looked all over, calling her name. No luck. We finally had to tell Mom. She wasn't a bit worried. I guess she figured Omega would turn up at supper time. She didn't. So Mom herself went over to the blue jeep camp and asked about her. The man was the same one she knew from Vernal. He didn't know what Mom was talking about. Said they hadn't seen any young girl. Double uuh!

Finally, Mom drove back to the Visitor Center to report Omega as missing. Jay-Rod and I stayed behind in case she should turn up. I asked Jay-Rod to use his indigo powers to try and locate her. He closed his eyes and tried. But he was "out" so long I got worried and had to shake him awake.

"C'mon, Buddy. What took you so long? What did you see?"

Jay-Rod shook himself awake and heaved a big sigh. "Yes. They've got Omega, all right. Some woman, not a man. In some cave around here. They want her buzzing Zuni necklace. She hid it somewhere. They're not letting her go until she tells them where. I'm going to find her."

Before I could even reply he was gone like a bat out of, you know where. It was dark by now, but Jay had the night vision of a bat. If anyone could find Omega it was Jay-Rod. But what was Mom going to say when she got back and found him gone, too. So I waited...and waited... and waited.

Finally Mom came back and we waited together. She was very angry that Jay-Rod had taken off like that. Like it was my fault that I didn't stop him. She should know nobody could stop Jay-Rod when he made up his mind.

I didn't tell her about Jay's vision of Omega with a woman in a cave. Mom didn't have much to say about whatever the park ranger told her. So we waited some more. It must have been close to midnight when we heard this racket—a car in low gear pulling up to our camp site with the seatbelt signal beeping like crazy. It was the blue jeep. And out popped the driver: Jay-Rod (whoa!) with a passenger, Omega.

Omega rushed into Mom's waiting arms, crying and laughing all at once. Jay-Rod yelled at me to get in the driver's seat and take the jeep back to the man's campsite. He'd show me where. So we did. I forgot to say that Jay could drive—sort of. I taught him secretly. But of course he was too young for a permit. How did he manage an SUV? Not very well, he admitted. He must have put it in four-wheel drive. And he didn't have time to buckle any seatbelt, so the stupid thing beeped all the way back.

Where were the man and woman? Back at the cave a few miles down the road. Or probably running this way. Jay first heard the man talking to the woman on his cell phone inside their tent. So he sneaked into the car and stowed away in the back area. Pretty soon the man got in and drove to the cave without even seeing Jay.

They shoved Omega into the car with the motor running, got out, and slammed the door. While they were outside arguing about what to do with Omega, Jay crawled up to the driver's seat and drove back here! Whoa! What a story! We left the jeep back at their camp so they couldn't accuse us of stealing it. Jay heaved the keys as far away as he could. But they probably had a second set.

"Let's get out of here, Mom!" he yelled when we got back to our camp. "We have to leave before they get back. I know they were running after me when I last saw them."

I was already tearing down the tent before Mom could be convinced we had to leave. She wanted to report those two to the park police for kidnapping. But I knew they were not going to believe our story. You know it! Adults never believe kids! It would end up being our fault, and Jay would go to jail for stealing their car! So we packed up and took off back up the road and stayed the night at a motel in Torrey. We hid the orange bus out back of the motel for good measure. Phew!

But Omega couldn't stop crying even after she got in bed. "I lost my Zuni necklace!" she sniffled. Mom said she would buy her another. (As if that would help!)

Finally Jay-Rod hopped over to her bed and whispered something in her ear: "Hold out your hand!" And there he put the necklace! She had taken it off and hid it in the way-back area of their SUV after they shoved her in the car. They were after the necklace and she couldn't think of where else to hide it. At least it wouldn't be around her neck. When Jay-Rod stowed himself away in the back area, he of course found it! But he found something else, too.

"What else did you lose, Omega?" Jay-Rod couldn't wait for her to find out. "Take a look in your neck pouch and see." She dumped it out, but there was the moldavite, safe and sound. We both thought that's what Jay-Rod had in mind. When he saw her moldavite his mouth dropped open. Then he opened up his hand and we could see why. There in his palm was another little piece of moldavite! Omygosh! He had found it on the floor of the way-back compartment where he found the Zuni necklace.

What's going on? What were those people doing with moldavite? How did that stone from the stars fit into the buzzing-rocks-and-necklace mystery? We took the two little modavite stones into the bathroom where we could examine them under a bright light without disturbing Mom. They looked alike except that Omega's piece was a little bigger.

"Come on, you kids. Time for bed." Mom rattled the bathroom door. "Save your talk for tomorrow. We've got petroglyphs to see in Capitol Reef and some great trails to hike. Let's get some sleep. You're safe again with us, Omega, and all's well that ends well," said Mom. But Jay whispered under his breath: "If it doesn't then it isn't the end."

We rolled our eyes, knowing it wasn't the end of it.

# 11

# Capitol Reef National Park: Petroglyphs

Once back at Capitol Reef Park we found a new campsite. No blue Jeep Liberty in sight. So over to the Petroglyph Walk boardwalk along the canyon cliffs we hurried. We were told that park rangers sometimes gave talks to groups about the petroglyphs on the cliffs there. Sure enough. There was a ranger on the boardwalk lounging in the shade of a big cottonwood tree waiting for a group to gather. Omega made herself right at home with him. He was an Indian! I didn't think Indians talked much. But this one poured out words like an avalanche on fire as soon as Omega approached. He didn't even wait for anybody else to gather. We had us our own private lecture—and not just about petroglyphs.

He started with all these questions: did we notice that most of the rocks in this canyon were red? Red was the color of the "root chakra." (Huh?) The color of Mother Earth. Did we know that this was the center of Mother Earth? Had we seen all the black volcanic rocks scattered around—in the shape of eggs? They're Mother Earth's eggs. (Whoa!) Did we notice all the domes? White people called them domes. Indians call them breasts. Mother Earth's breasts. Mother Earth was born here! (Oh-wow!)

This didn't sound very scientific. Was he a real ranger? Then he kept on about this place being sacred. "The first people who came here thousands of years ago knew it was sacred." He told us. "They carved pictures of themselves on the canyon walls. Today we call them petroglyphs. I'll show you." And he took us over to the railing as close as you could get to the petroglyphs on the canyon wall. (Not close enough for Jay).

I could feel Jay-Rod's energy building up. I quickly grabbed the back of his belt. Otherwise I knew he would go vaulting over the railing and scrambling up to the glyphs!

As the ranger continued talking he asked us to look closely at the images of the anthros carved into the cliffs.

A row of large anthros faced us like the ones at McKee and McConkie with broad shoulders and long bodies that tapered down into narrow waists with belts. Whoa! Their heads were square with earbobs and horned antennas on top that curved inwards, almost touching. At first glance I thought they were wearing round astronaut helmets! Yup. Stick arms with fingers at the end hung down from their shoulders. Stick legs were so short it made them look top-heavy.

"Do you think these are big?" asked the ranger. "Not as big as the huge Fremonts who came to Earth at McKee Springs or McConkie Ranch." He had seen those petroglyphs, too. They were the original ones. But they were named "Fremont" by an Anglo explorer who first discovered similar big petroglyphs right here by the Fremont River. That wasn't their real name. We don't know what it was, so we call them Fremont for the place where they were found.

"The Fremonts are guardians of the Earth," the ranger continued. "They came from the stars to bring star energy to balance the Earth. They were the culture bearers, too. They taught the natives how to find water, how to bring rain, how to grow plants in the desert, how to make pottery, and how to build houses. They were not warriors. Those first ones made pictures of themselves on these cliffs, so the natives would remember their teachings.

"After they were gone the natives made their own pictures of the Fremonts on rock walls in power spots all over the Southwest. The native people thought they were gods because of their large size and their power. I myself am a Zuni who still follows their teachings.

"Many Zuni and Hopi kachina ceremonies are based on the Fremonts—especially our ten-foot tall kachinas called *shalakos*," the ranger continued. "Some Zunis paint the weeping eye on the masks they wear for dancing. They got that from the pictures on the pouches the water-dowsing Fremonts carried. The native people were told to find Center Place to keep the Earth in balance. Some did. Some didn't. It is right here under our feet. Now it is time to balance the Earth once again."

We looked at him in wonder. Was he saying that this actual place was the Center Earth our petroglyphs told us to find? Then we had really found it without even trying! And "follow the rainbow?" The rainbow was the sleeping rainbow of colored rock layers in Capitol Reef National Park. Awesome!

Now the ranger eyed us with a stare that seemed to go right through us. "People with heart energy like yours need to put it back into the Earth at power spots. Star people cannot help this time. You have to do it yourselves. You need to go and find the power spots in this park. Green is the color of the heart chakra. Use green in your ceremonies."

Hoo-boy!

Then the ranger went over to Omega and gave her a "high five" with his hand. Only it wasn't a high *five*, but a high *three* because he had only three fingers just like Omega! Then he turned and walked away! Oh-wow! We were blown away! Who was that ranger? What did it all mean?

One thing we understood. We had really found Center Earth! Now we had to find the power spots in the park. How could we find them? Back at our campsite we got out booklets and maps of Capitol Reef to show us the park layout. We needed to know what its important features were and how we could get to them.

We spied one right away: the big white dome called Capitol Dome. It looked just like the capitol in Washington, DC. But how could we get up there? It didn't look like a very easy climb. Another power spot was surely the giant yellow monolith called the Golden Throne. Let's go there first, I told them. It looked like an easier climb. (Wrong).

To get there we would have to take the Capitol Gorge Trail on an old unused wagon road through a canyon. Then take a hiking trail up into the high country. Or maybe not. Couldn't we get a good view of the Throne from the canyon trail? Wouldn't that do? Who knows? Maybe some gold had dribbled down onto the road! (You know me). So off we went again in our orange bus, this time with Mom.

We drove past the Visitor Center and turned off at the buildings of the historical old Mormon town of Fruita, now in the center of the park; then past the old blacksmith shop to the Gifford House. We hadn't planned to stop, but Jay-Rod shouted "Whoa!"

It was more than just a pioneer home for tourists to visit. He could see people coming out with food in their hands. Little pies! Leave it to Jay. He could sniff out great things to eat anywhere. Yup. They were baking little fruit pies—cherry, apple, and peach from the orchards across the street! And you could buy little cups of ice cream to go along with them. Of course we stopped. And ate. And ate some more! We needed lots energy if we were going to hike, ya know!

Fruita was like a green oasis in this country of rainbow cliffs. Green meadows with deer grazing and orchards of fruit trees covered the flat valley floor. Behind them gigantic red-and-white striped cliffs loomed straight up 800 feet or more. Yikes! Red and white rock rubble lay in huge piles at their base. The rubble pieces were twice as high as the old Mormon barn nearby. I'm glad I wasn't around when those huge chunks of rock came thundering down from the cliffs. Even a little piece was bigger than our bus! Who could ever get through a mess like that, I'd like to know?

Luckily streams had cut their way through the mountains making canyons in places. Capitol Gorge canyon was one of the biggest. Still it was a squeeze where those walls closed in. They said it used to be the only road through the Waterpocket Fold before Highway 24 was built in 1962. What a rough ride, we imagined, as we climbed around rocks and waded through water. It used to be mostly flat until it got washed out in recent years, people told us.

Mom stayed at the head of the gorge to paint and wait for us to do our hiking. She had her eye on the bus, too. No more mysterious break-ins for her. So we entered the canyon where the sheer 800-foot cliffs on either side almost met together on the gorge floor. Just enough room for a wagon if you squeezed it. Yup. Some of the cliffs were mostly red. Some were white.

As we hiked around a curve, there it was. Through a break in the canyon walls we could see the Golden Throne. Awesome! It was a huge monolith of yellow Carmel Sandstone, towering above the canyon, glowing gold in the sun.

This was the spot for our ceremony, decided Omega. She was not about to climb the steep trail she noted to its top. So we did a ceremony right there in Capitol Gorge with cornmeal and tobacco. She even lit a little candle and blew the smoke up toward the Throne. "Okay, Darry. Now it's your turn. Let's have a chant!" Oh, man-o-man! Did I have to?

*Humm. Humm. Humm. Humm.*
*Feel our energy come, come!*
*Let our energy rise, rise!*
*Take it in and use it wise!*
*Humm. Humm. Humm. Humm. Ho!*

We clapped as we chanted. Some hikers eyed us suspiciously. This was getting embarrassing! I waggled two weak fingers at them, but then I perked up and directed, "Okay, let's everybody sing "Row, row, row, your boat!"

The hikers laughed and moved on. But somehow we couldn't seem to get going again. Omega remained seated on a rock and lowered her head. "We have to do something more in our ceremony. Remember, the Indian ranger said we should use green. Has anybody got any green on them?"

I stared at Omega. Oh, yeah. She knew what I was thinking because she was thinking the same thing. The moldavites. How could she part with either of them? Did I think the Indian ranger knew about her green moldavites? I nodded.

Okay. After a long pause she finally took one of the little green stones out of her pouch, wrapped it in a green leaf, and buried it under a rock near the opening in the canyon wall. I could hardly believe she would do that. It was a real sacrifice. Then we were able to move on. All but Jay-Rod. He still remained cross-legged on the ground meditating.

I took another quick peak way up at the Golden Dome. Did it really feel our energy? Something suddenly moved over the sun and a shaft of light streamed out and down from the Dome through the opening in the cliffs. And then it was gone. But the something was still there: a shining silver disk! Omygosh! A UFO…hanging right up there in the middle of the day! Doesn't anyone see it? Jay-Rod finally did. Omega did too. She waved and waved, jumping up and down. Hikers passed us by, glancing up, but not seeing anything. And then it was gone, too.

What was the matter with people? Their only interest was what they were doing, not what was going on around them. Too bad. Think of all they were missing! Jay-Rod never seemed to be missing anything not even when he was sitting cross-legged on the ground. Now what else was he after? Whoops! He almost got it. There!

He came up with this weird little flattened out lizard about the size of his hand with spines sticking out all over its back. Omygosh! He had a horny toad! This one was all puffed up and mad. I told Jay not to squeeze it so hard. Now it was puffing itself up to twice its size. "Mom told us they do that when they're being attacked. Don't you remember?" I reminded him. "It's a defensive mechanism." At least I learned something from Mom's home-schooling about desert animals.

"C'mon, put it down and let's go." I urged him. But he didn't. He said he had to take it with him for a special purpose. Hoo-boy! He said it had crawled right up onto his lap when he was meditating...that it was a Fremont ceremonial artifact. Oh, man-o-man!

He put the lizard in a little collecting box from his backpack. But that wasn't the end of it. Whenever it started scratching, he would let it out. Then it would scuttle over to the rocks along the canyon wall and stop. There would be a Fremont petroglyph for us to look at! I kid you not.

So that's the way it went for the rest of our hike. Hike, hike, scratch, scratch, scuttle, scuttle, stop. Hike, hike, scratch, scratch, scuttle, scuttle, stop. Thank the yowling universe there weren't many glyphs in the canyon, or we'd probably still be out there! Anyway, none of those Capitol Gorge petroglyphs was as big or clear as the ones along the boardwalk at Petroglyph Walk. I couldn't wait to get back there for another look at them.

Omega and Jay also wanted to get to the petroglyphs on the boardwalk along the Fremont River. But I think Jay really wanted to get out of that canyon in case that UFO decided to beam us up. So we hurried back to the bus. Should we tell Mom about the UFO? Probably not. She was so involved in her painting, nothing else much mattered. I drove back. She sat in back at the table, continuing to sketch.

When we finally got back to the boardwalk we could see those petroglyphs were much clearer than the ones in the gorge. We had seen some of them earlier with the Indian ranger. They showed large Fremont anthros standing in a row facing us with stick arms stretched down. Their five-fingered hands didn't holding anything like the dowsing pouches of the ones at McKee or McConkie.

Their square heads had ear bobs and curved horns on top. When I said that their curved horns made it look like the anthros were wearing astronaut helmets, Jay said they were! Their bodies were also filled in with no necklaces or decorations. Lots of bullet holes, though, from trigger happy cowboys, I guess.

We viewed them from that long boardwalk parallel to the cliff where we met the Indian ranger. You could look through binocular viewfinders like they have at Niagara Falls for a better view. I kept hold of Jay-Rod so he wouldn't take his own close-up look. (You know what I mean.) I think he was disappointed that they didn't have as much to say as the petroglyphs at McKee or McConkie.

"There's more of them buried under the rock fall at the base of the cliffs, Darry," he complained.

"What? How do you know?"

"They told me"

Wouldn't ya know it! I could just see him sneaking out at night with a shovel to dig them out. Shovel? Huh! It would take more than a backhoe to move those humungous rock slabs! But I was right. He did get more from the glyphs than he was letting on. Yup.

He told us that those anthros were captains sent out from a southern group of extraterrestrials. (Remember the upside down man?) They had to survey the land and lay it out for irrigation and planting. They were agricultural specialists sent to teach the native people how work the land. They set the rhythm for the work in the fields by *chanting*. What can I say? I was in good company.

We walked on down the boardwalk, using our own binoculars to scope out the glyphs through the cottonwood trees along the cliff. When the boardwalk ran out so did the petroglyphs. But we continued hiking along the road. Finally we came to the end of the cliff where the road turned. Suddenly scratch, scratch, scratch! The horny toad! Yup. It scuttled over to still another panel we hadn't noticed before.

Three of its anthros had breastplates with balls (communication devices). Their necklace strands showed their rank like stripes on a sergeant's arm. A single band headdress curved up from the top of their heads. It showed their connection to the Rainbow Order, declared Jay. "Guess what, guys. This panel is a control center in touch with their ship!"

Whoa! Then came a confusing panel of many glyphs. One was the top half of a Fremont with a large fancy headdress and breastplate. "The high commander of navigation. Name of Varug II. In charge of laying out a circular star map of the heavens. If you can believe it," said Jay-Rod, somewhat shakily. Wavy vertical lines of electrical energy seemed to rise up from bottom to top of the panel. There was even a swish above Verug II's head! Did he travel here with a dragon?

Omega went ahead scoping out all the glyphs. When she turned around she suddenly saw the entire white Capitol Dome in between the cliffs across the road! It stood out just like the Golden Throne in Capitol Gorge. Out came her candle, corn meal, and tobacco. Before we knew it another rock ceremony was under way. This time we chanted loudly and even danced since there was no one else around.

We almost drowned out the scratch, scratch, scratching from Jay-Rod's horny toad. He let it out of its box again and it suddenly scuttled across our path and into the brush before he could stop it. But there were no more petroglyphs to be seen anywhere. Whoa! Jay wanted to return the lizard to the place where he found it, but it was gone. We looked everywhere. How could it just disappear like that? In the end we decided it had finished its job here and "buried" itself, just like the buzzing rock in Joshua Tree National Park.

We turned again to the big white dome between the cliffs. I couldn't help thinking we might be too far away to make a difference with our ceremony. Also Omega refused to part with her second green moldavite as she had in our first ceremony. Suddenly a big black-and-white magpie swooped in and landed on a rock across the road, shrieking at us as if to say: "She heard you!" She? Yup. Jay-Rod said most of the rocks in this park were 'she's.'

A sudden beeping horn made us all jump. It was Mom in the bus, waving us all on board. She had news. She had met a man down in the campground who wanted her to follow him on over to Moab. Uuh! (What'd I tell you?) The whole place was dripping with petroglyphs for her to paint, he assured her. "There's even a mastodon! Your kids will love it! Or you can turn them loose in the awesome Arches National Park."

Moab, Utah? That's what we started out for, remember? But had we finished here with our energy work? Mom said we could always come back. Oh, man-o-man! Haven't I heard that song before? Then suddenly I heard another song—well, more like a whining "mag-mag-mag." What was that? Mom turned and said that it sounded like one of a magpie's quiet calls. But inside the bus? We looked all around but didn't see anything inside or out. Jay-Rod closed his eyes and nodded his head. Then he opened them and smiled. But he wasn't saying anything.

# 12

# Jarod's Turn

We left Capitol Reef National Park in such a hurry Darrell never got a chance to say that the people in the blue Jeep Liberty came back. I also saw their campsite over on the other side of the campground. We got out of there before they noticed us. I hope.

Omega is happy to come with us over to Moab. It will bring her closer to her home in Aztec, New Mexico. She had kept in touch with her father the whole time with her cell phone. He missed her and wanted all of us to *pay* him a visit. He is going to charge us heavily, he said! I hope we can convince Mom to go. He knows so much about the land and people of the Southwest. It would be great to see him again—and his wonderful Aztec ruins. He says he's the only ruin we will see.

We still don't understand about the moldavites. How did the blue jeep people get the one I found in their jeep? Why did they want it? Omega still has the one the Indian woman gave her. She never found another one even though she looked every place we stopped. She is not about to part with that stone until she finds more.

The Moab man told Mom there is a wonderful rock shop in Moab that will help her. And guess what, now the moldavite buzzes when she puts her Zuni pendant near it! "Oh, wow", as Darrell would say. Her pendant "phone" has been strangely quiet since we left Capitol Reef National Park. Maybe we're out of the Fremont's range.

Did we accomplish our mission to help balance Mother Earth by putting our energy into the power spots? Only time will tell. Darrell thinks we will need to return to Capitol Reef Park and finish the job. We didn't even look for the stone arches there that the Fremonts liked so much.

I think there may be other places around the Southwest that could also use our rock energy. Omega says she will contact the Native American spirits who know the land best of all. I laugh when I hear her say "Native American" because most real Indians don't use that term! She gives me a dirty look.

I wonder what happened to the ETs from the UFO at Taos? They said we'd be seeing more of them before we were through. I'm not sure I want to. At least we saw their ship. Darry thought it meant we weren't through yet. Will we ever be? Was Capitol Reef Park really Center Earth? Darry says we'll find out all the answers when our mission ends. If we don't find the answers, then it isn't the end. Hoo-boy, as he would say.

But I know a secret that nobody else knows. I think we took on a passenger when we got on the bus after Omega's last ceremony. Should I tell them? I think that big magpie who shrieked at us decided to come along—invisible of course. If Mom knew about it that would be the end. She's a bird lover but I wonder if she'd love a large, loud black-and-white bird character like a magpie inside the bus? Time will tell. Not me.

So we're finally on the road to Moab—or not!

# Glossary

Anglos: people of the white race

Archaeologist: scientists who study ancient civilizations and people

Artifact: found object that people made

Butte: flat-top mountain

Earth fault: Earth crack where earthquakes occur

Encyclopedia: a book or set of books containing all branches of knowledge in alphabetical order

Expedition: planned trip

Fiasco: disastrous happening

Flabbergasted: complete surprise

Hoax: pretense

Humungous: huge

Hustled: hurried

Implement: object used to make something work

Kachina: a holy being for Pueblo Indians; a messenger to the gods

Majestic: lofty, imposing, grand-looking

Mesa: plateau; flat-top raised earth

Motif: a recurring theme or idea in a literary, artistic, or musical work

Olfactory nerve: organ for smelling

Ostentatious: showy display

Rack: antlers of elk

Spasms: sudden muscular contractions

Stylized figures: figures shown in a particular artistic style; not natural

Tarantulas: large semi-poisonous spiders

Telepathic: words heard inside head

Transfixed: held motionless with amazement

Vaulting: leaping

Volcanic dike: long raised earth wall made by volcano

Wheedle: to try to influence someone with flattering words

# Bibliography

Houck, Rose. *Capitol Reef: Canyon Country Eden*. Torrey, UT: Capitol Reef National History Association, 1996.

Madsen, David B. *Exploring the Fremont*. Salt Lake City, UT: Utah Museum of Natural History, University of Utah, 1989.

Malotki, Ekkehart & Weaver, Donald E. *Stone Chisel and Yucca Brush: Colorado Plateau Rock Art*. Walnut, CA: Kiva Publishing, 2002.

Muensch, David & Schaafsma, Polly. *Images in Stone*. San Francisco, CA: Brown Trout Publishers, Inc., 1995.

Simms, Steven R. *Traces of Fremont: Society and Rock Art in Ancient Utah*. Salt Lake City, UT: University of Utah Press, 2010.

Slifer, Dennis. *Guide to Rock Art of the Utah Region*. Santa Fe, NM: Ancient City Press, 2000.

# Readers Guide

1. What are petroglyphs and why are there so many in Utah?

2. Why did Indians make petroglyphs? What do most people believe?

3. What was the importance of Jarod's hunting knife in this story?

4. How did Omega become involved with the boys? How did they feel about her?

5. How did UFOs become a part of this story? How did the characters feel about them"

6. What part did Omega's three fingers play in this story?

7. How did the McKee and McConkie petroglyphs differ from others the boys had seen?  Why were they important?

8. What do you think happened to Jay-Rod when he went into the crack in the McKee  cliff?

9. Who were the Fremonts? What did the boys find out about them?

10. What did "follow the rainbow" and "find Center Earth" mean?

11. What did the occupants of the blue Jeep Liberty want from Omega? Why?

12. How did the boys and Omega help the Earth in Capitol Reef National Park?

CPSIA information can be obtained
at www.ICGtesting.com
Printed in the USA
BVHW011834130621
609475BV00014B/505